# SAORSA

### KERRY HEAVENS
### HEATHER SHERE

Vickie
Find your Sdorsa
Kerry Heaven

Heather Shere

HEAVENS & SHERE

SAORSA

ISBN: 9781798918579

Cover Image: Rplusmphoto
Cover Models: Connor Smith & Jess Epps
Cover Design: Rebel Graphics
Editing: Virginia Tesi Carey
Proofing: Mandi Gibala
Formatting: Rebel Graphics

*For Betty*

SAORSA

[*seer-sha*]

**Noun -** Scottish Gaelic

Freedom, salvation, redemption, liberty.

# ONE

I have waited six long years for this moment. To be free.

My lawyer and I are already seated at the table when he enters the boardroom; we were here first on purpose. I have my laptop, pen and pad of paper all squarely lined up, to send the message that I am prepared. I don't plan on using any of them.

They enter the room chuckling, probably at some off-humor joke. He pauses when he sees me already sitting here, the smile rapidly leaving his face. He glances at his lawyer, who has wiped the smile off his face too and then looks back to me, his momentary off-guard expression rapidly replaced by his standard over-confidence.

"Charlotte, it's good to see you," he says smoothly, crossing the room. Reluctantly, I stand. He leans in, kissing the air by my cheeks. "You look beautiful as always," he tells me softly, always employing charm to get what he wants even when the negotiations are over. I deserve a best actress award for not cringing.

"Henry," I greet him, my voice monotone as I incline my head and sit back down. Of course he thinks I'm beautiful, I have the so-called timeless look he favors. Long blonde hair I always wear in a classic French twist, sage green eyes, and I was blessed with a soft but slender hourglass figure. All the superficial things matter so much to him but so little to me. I am more than my looks and he never appreciated that.

"Mrs. Cole," his lawyer greets me, shaking my hand.

"Ms. Rose," I correct with a dash of venom.

His face flushes slightly and he nods apologetically, then greets my lawyer hurriedly to move on from his mistake. Once the false pleasantries are over, I turn to retake my seat.

My Chief Operating Officer and dear friend, Edward's, words to me before I entered the room still repeat in my ears. "Are you sure you want to do this, Charlotte?"

It is the third time he's asked me today and the hundredth this week. He wants me out of this toxic situation as much as I do, but he also knows that letting go is going to be hard for me. He's well aware that the deal on the table is insulting and yet the best I'm likely to ever get.

I gave him a reassuring smile to ease his torn conscience, before promising him I was more than ready for this all to be over. I told him to go back to work, but I'll bet he's out in the foyer right now, wearing a groove in the plush carpet.

I put Edward out of my mind before I lose my nerve and straighten my suit jacket, folding my hands and resting them on the table. I'm ready.

Henry has a slimy smirk on his face as he takes his seat, the one that says he knows he's screwing me. I've put up with him for far too long, my stubbornness was willing to wait him out for a better deal, but I'm done. Every month spent negotiating is a month of my life wasted and I will be happier when I'm free. For once in my life, I have reached a place where the idea of freedom, of happiness, outweighs the need to hold on to this life and what I'm owed from it.

I wait for my lawyer to take the lead, showing no emotion at all. It's a skill I have perfected over the years, unlike Henry who can barely contain his giddiness.

"Shall we get started then?" he blurts. The fool has no clue of the fall that's coming to him. Watching him practically bouncing in his seat, I can't believe I was married to him for ten years. I was so in love with him at eighteen and completely blind to who he was...is. Married fresh out of high school, it had been happy to begin with, or so I thought. I was so dumb when I think back on it now, taking any jobs I could to support us while we put ourselves through college.

I did everything I could to keep us afloat while he did so little. The focus was always on his education, when in fact it was me who worked hard in and out of class. My skill that got us off the ground, my patience that made us a success, and my passion and commitment that put together the best team. Without me he would be...well, I guess he's about to find out.

We built this financial firm together, started it with just us and now we employ over five hundred people. Our plan was to ultimately go international but I stopped pushing for it when our relationship began to fall apart. Now, I'm walking away from it all. Let him see how much of this company is my doing once he has to fend for himself.

My lawyer interrupts my thoughts by passing out the contracts. "Mr. Cole has already agreed to the terms. We are here today to make this thing official and go on our merry way."

Henry offers him his best 'We'll see about that' smile and thumbs through the contract. "You're sure, Charlotte?" he says in his patronizing way, not even bothering to look at me. "You sure you can agree not to start a firm in any of the states we already have offices and the sanctions on our client list preventing you from working with any present client or their subsidiaries for the next ten years?"

I watch him skim pages he has had in his possession for

weeks. He really thinks he has me. He's so convinced I will want to set up in direct competition with him that his whole negotiation strategy has been centered on crippling my chances of doing so and therefore keeping me where I am, building our company up, for him.

"Of course," I reply, sounding as innocent as I can manage. "With this kind of money, I could retire at thirty-four."

His eyes snap up to mine, surprise at my words registering on his face. He knows I live to work, so the very idea of me retiring so young, I'm sure, shocks the shit out of him. The consummate businessman he is, quickly catches himself expressing surprise and his features change instantly. Heaven forbid anyone catches the great Henry Cole off-guard!

He tries to turn the tables and his eyes become soft, I know his cajoling tone is coming. It's a gift he has always had, being able to turn on that boyish charm from when we were young, the one I fell for a lifetime ago. It doesn't work anymore, but it's cute when he tries. "You could have stayed at home while we were married." His voice is full of regret. He always wanted that. Him in the boardroom making the millions, me at home making...I don't know what...gourmet food and babies probably. I barely contain my shiver of revulsion. He may have wanted that, but he would have none of this if I had been at home with two point five kids. I am this company.

"You have your current wife for that, Henry," I point out flatly, emphasizing the word 'current', because we both know that now that he's popped his divorce cherry, there's no stopping him.

His face flushes in annoyance and he audibly growls. His lawyer elbows him and points to where he needs to sign on the document, hoping to move things along before Henry blows the deal for himself. He presses his lips together in a firm line as his scribbles his name like a five-year-old across the contract. His lawyer signs as a witness and then pushes it across the table back to mine. I inwardly smile as he makes a big show of checking every page is signed, even though I know he was counting signatures as they were signing them. Always looking out for me.

"Ms. Rose, I need you to sign and initial where I marked the red x's." He passes me the contract.

I nod. I don't need to read the contract again. We've gone through this with a fine-tooth comb. Henry is outright buying my half of the business. In the six or so years since we have been divorced, he has consistently run the business into the ground on purpose. His motive was precisely this moment, where he took everything over for less than it was worth. But the joke is on him, I'm walking away because I'm ready, not because the value has dropped.

I could have done this years ago in the divorce settlement, but I didn't want to give up my baby then. Not when I had worked so hard to build it and took so much joy from it. Besides, I could tolerate him for the sake of my one true love. Now, it is time. I have plans of my own, plans for myself.

I sign my name with a flourish, my penmanship flawlessly feminine yet strong and controlled. I push the contract back and he signs his sections and lets Henry's lawyer review it. He nods his head after he is done, smiling with smug satisfaction. "Cole Financial is now one hundred percent yours," he tells Henry. "Congratulations." He shakes Henry's hand, while I grit my teeth.

My lawyer clears his throat. "Before you celebrate, have the funds been deposited in Ms. Rose's account?"

Henry's eyes widen slightly, offended by the question. "Is my word nothing anymore, Charlotte? We agreed I would transfer it first thing this morning."

"Don't get your panties in a bunch, Henry. He's just looking out for my best interests," I scold, opening up my laptop and logging into my bank, the silence in the room not intimidating me one bit. I see the balance and smile.

"The funds are there. We are done here." I snap my laptop closed with a loud click.

"Perfect." Henry claps. His lawyer stands, filing away their copies of the paperwork. Henry quickly follows. Now that he has secured his victory he can't wait to get out of the conference room, but I still have one or two things to discuss with him.

"Henry, before you go, could I just have a word?"

Our lawyers exchange a glance and Henry looks imploringly at his, but I dismiss them. "It's okay, this is a private matter. You two can go." I take my seat again and watch as Henry considers bolting, but reluctantly returns to his chair as the lawyers shuffle out, not even closing the door behind them.

I stare at him for a moment, not knowing if I'm delighting in or hating the idea of delivering the final blow. But I'm committed now, there is no going back. I square my shoulders and meet his eyes. "You'll find my office is cleared out already," I inform him. "And here is my laptop and phone." I set my cell on top of the laptop and slide it forward. "I'm leaving, effective immediately."

"B-but..." he chokes. "You were going to stay on for a while, to wrap up the things you were working on." He clenches his fist on the table.

"I no longer have a vested interest in the company, Henry." I lift my bag from the floor and slide my notebook and pen neatly inside, leaving everything else where I left it. I stand and smooth down my shift dress.

"But, Charlotte—" Henry leaps to his feet, coming around the table to stop me leaving, when a knock on the half open door pulls our attention from each other.

Edward stands in the doorway, his eyes searching me for some sign of my wellbeing.

"This is not a good time, Edward," Henry snaps, barely looking in his direction.

I nod faintly to Edward so he knows I'm alright, that everything went as we expected and can leave me rather than face Henry's wrath, but he stands firm.

"I'm sorry to interrupt, but I'm afraid this won't wait."

Henry exhales sharply and folds his arms. "What is it then?" he demands.

Edward slips into the room and takes an envelope out of the inside pocket of his jacket handing it purposefully to Henry. "My resignation, Mr. Cole. I'm sorry for the short notice but today will be my last day."

I look between Henry and Edward calmly, keeping the shock from showing on my face as this wasn't part of my plan. Edward has a small smirk playing about his lips, he knows damn well he just gave me a jolt.

Henry's face is a shade of reddish-purple that I haven't seen since I agreed with him that we should divorce. As he'd tried to use it as a threat in an argument, the last thing he expected was for me to agree with him.

"But you're in the middle of the Wake deal," he shouts incredulously.

Edward shrugs semi-apologetically. "I can't work for someone I don't respect."

It takes all of my poise not to snort with laughter. Henry just doesn't comprehend that I'm the glue that has held this company together since the beginning. He's going to lose more than Edward in the long run, he just doesn't know it yet.

Henry stares at the unopened envelope for what seems like forever, then he seems to gather himself and fixes us both with a frigidly resentful glare. "In that case, I'd like you both to leave the building immediately. I'll call someone to escort you out. We'll have someone in maintenance pack up your things and ship them to you, Edward. I'm sure you understand," he sneers.

Edward barks out a laugh, a rare show of his 'off duty' side. "Henry, you have turned into a little prick, I wouldn't stay a minute longer if you offered me ten times my salary. You'll find my office in the same fashion as Charlotte's, cleared out with my laptop and phone on my desk. There won't be a need to ship anything and we can see ourselves out. Now, if you'll excuse us." He offers his elbow to me to me. "Shall we?"

Knowing it will piss Henry off, I slide my hand around his arm and give him a smile. "Yes, we shall. Let's go to lunch."

Henry's panicked voice booms across the room as we leave. "Charlotte, how can I contact you if I need you? You've left your phone."

I pause, looking back over my shoulder. "Precisely. We no longer have any connection. Have a wonderful life, Henry. I know I will." Without a second thought, I walk out of the board-room, with my head held high.

We step out of the elevator to the main lobby and I stop dead when I find everyone I've personally hired over the years has gathered and are clapping their hands for me. It was common knowledge what was going down here today, that I was signing off. But word must have gotten out that I was also leaving for good today. I side-eye Edward who simply shrugs. I had briefed everyone personally about the change of ownership, I wanted to make sure all of my people, my coworkers, knew that they weren't the reason I sold out. My jaw tightens as I think about the term 'sell out'. I really didn't have a choice. I made certain the coworkers were all taken care of. I wrote letters of recommenda-tions for a few people who had expressed a desire to move on after I left and gave my personal information to others. But I was not expecting this. I was expecting to just slip quietly out of the door.

I feel that tickle you get in your throat when you're going to cry and remember an old trick I was taught by my mentor. She told me if you ever feel like you're going to cry at a moment you need to stay professional, to do math problems in your head. I start with little problems, one plus one and work my way up in numbers as I make my way through the crowd, shaking hands.

The senior managers are waiting by the front door, and they place a bouquet of flowers in my arms. I turn back to all the people I have worked with for so long and swallow hard. A hush falls.

"Thank you, everyone. Words can't express how much you all mean to me." I clutch the flowers to my chest. These people were my family, my children per se. "I really will miss you all." My voice threatens to crack, so I press my lips together.

"Are you ready, Charlotte?" Edward asks with his hand on my arm to direct my attention to him.

"Yes." I look to Jennings, our operations manager, and nod to the gathered crowd. "You'd better get them back to work, he's going to be a dick all day."

He waves the crowd off, and they start to disperse, heading back up to their cubicles.

"Sweetheart, he won't do anything to them. The competition has been headhunting here ever since it came out that you were leaving. If he doesn't watch out, he'll lose more than a handful." He laughs and walks with us outside of the building.

I ordered a car to bring me in and wait for the meeting to be over, and I find it waiting right where I left it. "Edward are you coming with me or did you drive in?" I stop where the chauffeur is standing with the door open.

"We're both coming with you." Edward motions to the car with a grin.

"You both quit?" My mouth falls open in surprise.

"Yes, he will find my letter on my desk." Jennings snickers.

"But, what are you going to do?" My brows furrow with concern.

"Oh darling, who do you think the headhunters got to first?" Jennings throws his head back in a wicked laugh.

I can't hold my giggle back. "So we all need to go celebrate?"

"Yes, after you, dear." Jennings puts his hand out directing me into the car.

I turn and look at the empire we built from the ground up, and I'm surprised that I don't feel any regrets. I lift my chin up. I did everything I could. I look at Jennings and Edward, their grins matching my own.

"Let's go, gentlemen." I step into the limousine first.

The driver pulls away and I keep my head facing forward.

Never look back, Charlotte.

# TWO

Checking the world clock on my phone, I see it's midnight in London. I had refrained from telling her that today was the day. She would want to run to my side and, well, her job doesn't just let her leave on a whim. I open our iMessage chat and ponder for a few seconds before I send her a text.

**Me:** You awake?

I hit send and stare at the screen. In true Louise fashion, it takes only a few seconds before I see the message go to 'read' and the little pop up tells me that she's typing. Then a full minute passes before her reply comes through.

**Louise:** Yes.

**Me:** It took you a whole minute to type yes?

Another minute goes by as she types.

**Louise:** Apparently. She also sends the eye roll emoji.

**Me:** Sausage finger typing?

I sit back with a grin. Even with significant news like this, I can't resist the temptation to tease her. It's the little things in life I enjoy.

**Louise:** Bitch! She says a minute later.

I snicker and decide to stop playing with her. I look around the living room at all the packed boxes. Most of it is going into storage, since I don't have another place just yet, but I'm taking everything I need for the short-term. I hit the FaceTime option on my phone and wait for the three rings before she picks it up.

"Hello?" Her proper, sing-song British accent always makes me smile.

"Hi. Did the phone drop on your face?" I squint my eyes trying to see if that's a shadow I see, or a red spot on her forehead.

"Yes, I was scrolling Tumblr and you scared me. What's going on? You didn't warn me you were going to call. I look wretched." She tries to smooth out the frizzes sticking up on her hair.

"Oh shut your mouth. You always look beautiful," I tell her, taking a sip from my glass of wine as she rolls her eyes.

"So is everything okay? You hardly ever call." She sits up in bed bringing the phone closer to her face.

I smile into the phone. I can see from the corner picture how happy I look.

"Spill!" she demands, her eyes like saucers.

"I'm free." I grin even wider, if that's even possible. My face feels like it's going to break.

"I know." Her face falls with disappointment and she rolls her eyes again. "You got divorced years ago."

"No, I mean the paperwork was signed this morning." I pause and watch her, waiting for my words to make sense.

"Wait, what? I thought that there wasn't a date yet, that you kept pushing it off for more?"

"I may have fibbed just a teeny tiny bit." I pinch my forefinger and thumb together giving her the visual.

"You did this on purpose so that I wouldn't worry." She frowns at me.

I shrug, not feeling one ounce of guilt. It was for my sanity more than hers. "It was better this way."

"Jesus, Charlotte, we didn't make any plans." She flips the covers off her and jumps out of bed.

"What kind of plans?" I am a horrible friend, because I think this is all very funny.

"What are you going to do?" she asks dramatically. "I mean, I know you're going to be set for money, but you need to work or you'll go insane."

"I'll drive you insane you mean?" I cackle. She gives me a look that says 'yes, exactly that'. "Slow down, Louise. We have time," I tell her, getting a kick out of her reaction. Anyone would think we were married, but no, what we have is better than marriage. She is my best friend in the whole world. She just gets me.

"When is your last day in the office?" she asks, her wheels visibly turning as she starts to make emergency plans in her mind that she will never need to put in place.

"It was today," I tell her slowly for effect.

"What?" Her eyes bug out. This is almost as fun as making Henry squirm.

"Did you find another job already? Damn it, Charlotte, we need to sort your shit out."

"I might have found a job. I have an interview in three days."

I see her visibly relax. "Oh thank goodness."

One of the good things about living so far away is she doesn't know everything that I do.

"Aren't you going to ask me where?" I truly am a horrible person, I know my words prod her like a hot poker.

"If it's not here, it doesn't really matter, does it?" she sulks.

"Well..." I tease.

"Shut the front door! You're not serious?" Her voice rises.

I reach over and pick up my second surprise and say nothing

as I hold it up for the camera. I hold it steady so she can really get a good look at the color and lettering.

"A British passport? Oh my God! Are you freaking kidding me?" she screams.

"You're going to wake your neighbors," I scold.

"I don't care, the wankers were up all night last night having a party. So...this is actually happening? You aren't playing with me?" She paces her bedroom as she peppers off the questions.

I look out across my living room and see all the boxes, stacked and labeled, containing my belongings. Everything I own, all packed up neatly. The excitement of this new adventure gives me little butterflies in my belly.

I turn my phone around. "I don't know. Does that seem real?"

"Oh shit," she gasps.

I flip the phone back to me. "I'm coming, Louise."

"When are you coming to me?" She goes to clap excitedly and forgets she is holding her phone and drops it onto the carpet.

I laugh hard. "My flight leaves tomorrow night." I hold the phone away from my face in anticipation of her scream.

"Oh my God!" She yells so loud into the phone there is a static sound that comes from the speaker.

"Calm down, Louise."

"I have to straighten up. I'm going to be up all night cleaning," she whines.

"Don't bother. I can help you."

"I don't know if I can get Wednesday off." Her eyes go wide at the thought.

"I'm not worried about that. I can just order a car when I get there."

"I will get it off, even if I have to call in sick." She presses her lips in a tight line and has a stubborn tilt to her head.

"I have the shipping company coming tomorrow morning to pick up most of my things. I'll be putting it in storage there."

"You have everything set, don't you?" she asks, shocked.

"I do. Aren't you proud of me?" Seeing her face right now makes me so happy that in just a couple of days time we will be sitting across from each other.

"I want to wring your neck and then hug you."

"I will allow you one hug." I nod firmly and give her a sly smile.

"I'll give you as many hugs as I damn well please." She yawns.

"What time do you have to be at work tomorrow?"

"Eight." She covers her mouth as she yawns again.

"Go to bed. I just couldn't wait until morning to tell you."

"Okay, I will talk to you before you get on the plane. I still can't believe you will be here this week."

"For good! I'll be living there, just like we always wanted. I'll talk to you tomorrow."

"Bye, love you." She blows kisses into the phone.

I roll my eyes, laughing and end the call.

The doorbell to my condo rings, making me jump. I automatically look over at where my clock used to hang and find only bare wall. Instead, I pick my phone back up and see that it's seven thirty pm. The doorbell rings again, a couple more times in fact. Ugh, who does that? Teenagers maybe?

"I'm coming, hold your horses," I yell as I walk to the door.

I swing it open and groan, wishing I had looked through the peephole first.

"Hello, Henry, to what do I owe this pleasure?" My sarcastic tone falls on deaf ears. I stand at the door, blocking his entry.

"I wanted to talk to you." His eyes dart from side to side.

"About what?"

"Aren't you going to invite me in?" He tries to look over my shoulder and I stop fighting the urge to keep him in the dark. He's going to find out some time.

Sighing I walk back into the living room, leaving the door open for him to follow. "Make it quick."

"Why is everything packed up?" He looks around as he steps into the foyer. "Are you going somewhere?"

"You always were astute, Henry," I deadpan. "I'm moving, now what's up? I have a bunch of things I need to take care of." I barely contain the need to tap my foot in annoyance.

"I want you to come back." He shuffles his feet and can't look me in the eye.

I can't stop the mirthless laugh that bursts forth.

"I need you, Charlotte," he pleads, running a hand through his hair, his weariness showing in the lines etched on his face.

"You only think you need me, Henry. You couldn't wait for me to sell. Why are you even here?" I cross my arms, waiting to hear what fresh nonsense spills out of his mouth.

"I only wanted to own the company outright, because..." He rests a hand on the back of his neck looking up.

"Because the new, improved Mrs. Cole was having a hissy fit about you being business partners with the ex, right? It's okay, Henry, everyone knows what's going on here. You don't need to pretend anymore. I wasn't going to bow out to placate a spoiled child, you knew that. I sold because the time is right for me to move on."

"But the company needs you." He sounds desperate. More so than I had envisaged. It has only been hours, surely he hasn't fucked it all up already.

"You knew I was going, we agreed," I remind him.

"We agreed you would see out your projects," he snaps.

"And what difference would a couple more weeks really make to you, Henry? You got what you wanted, you'll have to step up and make it work on your own eventually, why delay the inevitable?"

Henry hangs his head. "I was hoping, once the deal was done

and the animosity was put aside, I'd be able to convince you to stay on. I'd pay you double if I had to, I just need you to stay."

I almost feel sorry for him. He has fucked himself and he is just starting to realize it.

"I'm sorry, you made your choice when you let your wife start making the calls from behind the scenes. I can't be a part of that. It's your company now and there is no place for me there."

"Charlotte, you're what makes everything run smoothly. It's all falling apart now." He starts pacing.

"What did you expect? Do you think the staff don't know how bad you fucked me in the deal?" I feel no guilt, he got exactly what he wanted.

"You weren't supposed to disclose anything about the deal. You signed a nondisclosure agreement." His voice starts to rise as he stops his pacing to glare at me.

This makes me laugh. "It doesn't take a rocket scientist to figure it out. They see how poorly you treated me. The business was my baby—not yours—and you didn't care."

"That's not true."

"Come on now, Henry, we've been at this ever since you remarried. For years I've been willing to sell you my half at market value, but you...or probably that little brat you call a wife...didn't think I deserved what it was worth. No, you thought you could ruin office morale, undermine my integrity with the big clients and run my baby into the ground. Then when it was all only barely holding together, undercut me and take everything for far less than is fair," I scoff. "You are more naive than I thought if you think no one at the company noticed."

"That was all business. I made some bad choices." He fumbles for excuses. "I know the firm means just as much to you. Will you please come back and work for me? I was serious, I'll double your salary," he says in a desperate, pleading tone.

"That's where you are wrong. I no longer care about *your*

business, my name isn't tied to it anymore. I'm ready to take on a new challenge." I watch the ugly snarl forming on his face and can't believe I was married to him for so long.

"God damn it, Charlotte!"

"Watch your tone, Henry," I say as calmly as possible. I know his stages of regret, they slowly turn into stages of rage.

"You have to come back." His eyes plead.

"Sorry, I came to terms with selling my half to you. I no longer have an investment in the company." I shrug and know deep down I don't care what happens to the company. It's a freeing thought.

"All of the managers quit," he blurts.

I stifle a laugh. I guessed more would follow Edward, but all of them? "I had heard rumors some would leave, did you expect any less?"

"Yes! I expected things to carry on as normal." He starts his pacing back up, waving his hands in the air as he stumbles over his words.

"*I* built that team and *I* kept them together," I remind him, my voice raising more than I wanted it to. "You were a fool to think they would stay, knowing how you screwed me over."

"They didn't even give me notice." His nostrils flare as he tries to control his rage.

"You did nothing to make sure they stayed. You knew this day was coming for weeks and yet, you were too good to have personal conversations with them, weren't you?" I'm getting tired of him in my space. This was also our home for many years and he feels too comfortable here. It's starting to turn my stomach.

"I had communications out. If anyone had any questions, they were free to contact me."

"A company wide memo? Very personal, Henry. Shows you really care."

He clenches his jaw, and his face turns a few different shades of red as he opens his mouth and closes it again.

"Was there anything else? I have a lot to take care of before my move."

He rushes over and grabs my upper arms, giving me a quick shake.

"You have to help me," he begs.

"No, I don't. Take your hands off me." I could physically try to shake him off me but I want him to realize for himself that he is taking things too far.

As the realization dawns, he opens his hands and holds them up, looking at them like he doesn't know how they got there. "I'm sorry. I'm just desperate."

"You should have thought of all this before it got this far."

"You were always the planner," he admits with a sigh and scrubs his hand over his face.

"Yeah well, I stopped planning on your behalf a long time ago." Thank fuck, I think to myself, never more glad he is someone else's problem now.

"Come on, Charlotte, we were so good together," he murmurs in what he thinks is a sexy voice.

"Stop. We don't need this trip down memory lane. What we had died long ago."

"How about you just stay for another month and help me repair the damage? I'll make it worth your while and everyone else's that chooses to come back. We could make this company great again." His eyes look like a wounded puppy's as he tries to bargain.

"Sorry, those little tricks with your eyes don't work with me anymore," I inform him.

"Where are you moving to? I can help you and we can talk about the business."

"I am leaving New York. Time to move on to something fresh and exciting."

"Going to Jersey? I can get a car and help."

He gets a few points for effort, but no.

"No, I am moving to be near Louise." A huge smile spreads across my face.

"But—" He chokes then sputters. "She lives in London."

"I am well aware of that." My reply is sarcastic, but the truth of it makes me giddy.

"You can't just move there. You're an American, you'll need a visa, a job, a sponsor!" He scoffs and crosses his arms knowing he's made an unarguable point.

"You really never paid attention to my family did you, Henry?" I sigh.

"You were an only child." He frowns. "Your parents were divorced, your Mom killed herself the first year we were married. What else is there?"

"My father? My heritage? Do you recall any of that?" I shake my head and watch his face as he tries to remember.

"He died when you were a child. I don't see where this is going." He shrugs.

"He was born in England."

"Okay, so?"

I can't believe I married this man. I was young and oh so dumb.

"Because he was British and married to my mother when I was born, I am entitled to British citizenship. I'm an American, yes. And also, now a Brit. I got all my documentation through a week ago, but that's enough about my business."

"So that's it? You won't even think of coming back?" He runs a hand through his hair.

"Nope. Now if there isn't anything else you need, I really need to get back to my list of things to do."

He nods, defeated and turns toward the door, then pauses. He doesn't face me when he asks, "Will you at least talk to Edward and Jennings for me? If they changed their minds, I know others would follow."

"No, you made your bed. This is what you wanted, remember? To call all the shots by yourself. This is your mess, you made it, you can regret it."

His head is bowed and he doesn't turn to look at me as he lets out a long exhale. "You're my biggest regret, Charlotte," he says softly.

"I could say the same," I whisper.

He turns quickly, his eyes round with shock and closes the few feet between us, throwing an arm around my waist, pulling me close.

It is at that moment I realize he doesn't see that we both meant our words in different ways. He leans in in slow motion, his face getting closer and closer to mine. Oh my God, he is going to try and kiss me! I raise a hand and put my palm to his forehead to stop his descent on my mouth.

"I don't think your *wife* would like this situation," I state calmly.

He stills and his face flushes red, he takes a step back. "I'm sorry, I need to go."

"I think that's best."

He looks down at the floor and then turns and takes the few steps to the door. He puts a hand on the knob and pauses, he turns back toward me. "Will you give me your new contact information?"

"I think it's best if we just cut ties." As the words slip from my lips, I feel like a ton of bricks has been lifted off my shoulders. I have always wanted to say that but was afraid that once I admitted it to myself, that I might be wrong, that maybe he was always the only one.

He isn't. I know that now more definitely than I have ever known it.

"I thought you'd say that, you're a hard woman, Charlotte," he delivers the parting shot and opens the door.

"Have a great life, Henry. I know I plan to," I say as he closes the door behind him. I refrain from running to the door, opening it and shouting some scathing remark. Him calling me hard is just because he never could handle a strong independent woman. He has a little wife at home now, he should be happy. I turn back to my living room full of boxes. My reminder that I just closed the door on my old life and I'm about to fling open the door to my new life.

# THREE

An electric excitement builds in my belly as we deplane. I can't wipe the smile off my face no matter how exhausted I am. I've been through this terminal plenty of times when I used to come over to visit Louise, so I know exactly where to go. We all file out like cattle and head to the packed customs area, only this time I get to go into a different line.

I follow the signs for the British passport line, the accents all around me comforting. The line moves quickly, not like when I would have to use the line for my American passport.

My palms are sweaty and I look around, watching to see how people just hand over their documents and move forward. Nothing life-changing in their actions, just a tedious part of their traveling experience. My nerves are on edge; this feels like I'm doing something wrong. I suppress a sound of nervous excitement. I'm up next! I hand my new passport over and the Customs official opens it at the photo page, checks my picture against my face and then scans it through his computer without showing any kind of emotion. He has no clue how important this moment is to me.

Once he has completed his checks, he closes my passport and hands it back to me, finally looking at me with a smile. "Welcome home," he says warmly.

I can only return his smile. *Home,* I think to myself as I move on to baggage claim.

When I walk through those double doors, my eyes scan the crowd looking for vibrant red hair. Once I'm clear of the exit walkway, I stop and get my cell phone out, turning it on. It takes a few seconds while it syncs up to the new country and a message pops up.

**Louise:** Stuck in traffic. I'll be there soon. Xx

I shrug slightly at her text, I expected it. The girl will be late to her funeral.

**Me:** K

Texting her back one letter gives me satisfaction because it annoys her. I can just hear her huff and see the eye roll. I bet she even presses her foot down on the gas pedal to go faster. Anyway, I don't mind, it gives me a few extra minutes to go into my first stop whenever I arrive.

I walk into the airport branch of Pret and the cashiers take my order, then quickly move on to the next customer with the same smile. I find a seat and park my luggage beside me so I can take my time with my coffee and pastry while I wait for Louise. I know I have a good half hour before she even gets to the airport. I love Louise dearly, but she is always late, I had to learn to accept that years ago.

I peel off a crispy piece of the croissant and take a bite, closing my eyes as the buttery flavor melts in my mouth. Something about the dairy is richer in the UK. It makes everything creamier, butterier, crispier...just...better. Who am I kidding? Everything is better over here.

"Do you mind if I share your table?" a deep, Scottish accent asks above me. It sounds like how I would imagine a finely aged whiskey would have if it spoke.

I look up and words fail me. Instead of replying, I nod meekly and incline my head as the Scottish dream sits down across the table from me. Dark hair, blue eyes, and a full-on beard. He sets his arms on the small table and I notice a tattoo crawling up his forearm under the pulled back sleeve of his shirt. His hair is long enough on top to be tied back effortlessly, but the sides shaved close. He has west coast hipster written all over him, but his Scottish accent squashes that thought right away. He's easy on the eyes, though not my type at all. I'm more of a clean-cut businessman kind of girl.

"My apologies for barging in and interrupting what looks to be the murder of a fantastic croissant. It's just, seats are at a premium here and I'm knackered." He gives me a charming smile.

I swallow and stare. His voice is a little more elegant than his appearance. "It's fine, I don't mind."

"Thank you. What part of the States are you from?" he inquires, taking a sip from his Pret cup.

"New York, is it that obvious?"

"That you're American? Yes. But I wouldn't have placed you from New York though." He sits back and studies me for a moment.

"No? Where would you place me then?" I don't have a strong New York accent, seeing where people put me has always been a fun game for me.

"I don't know, but your accent is more refined than most New Yorkers I've met."

I laugh. "I took speech lessons in high school so I wouldn't have that accent. Sometimes it's ear piercing." I finish up the last of my pastry, almost tempted to get another one. I didn't eat any of the in-flight meals.

"Understandable, you come across the same thing here. The farther north you go the harder it is to understand people."

"I will have to remember that." I look down at my watch and see that twenty minutes have passed. "It's been lovely chatting with you, I need to go meet my friend," I tell him, getting to my feet.

"Thank you for sharing your table," he says, standing in a gentlemanly gesture.

"No problem, you have a lovely day." I smile, pushing my cart away from the table.

"You too," he replies. "Miss...?"

I choose to appear not to hear his question. I'm far enough away to have not heard him and I don't really want to get into a conversation about my marital status with a stranger, however beautiful he is. Louise would be trying to get me to stay and have a chat with him, but he really isn't my cup of tea.

I leave the coffee stop and see her from across the terminal looking for me. Her head goes down, and she stops walking. This is her texting stance and a moment later, my phone buzzes in my pocket, so I pull it out.

**Louise:** I'm here!

I can feel her excitement through the text.

**Me:** I see you.

I add the crying laughing emoji and hit send.

I know the second she reads the message because she goes on tiptoes and starts searching the crowd with more urgency. I hunch over, so I appear smaller in the group and start pushing the cart in her direction. Louise isn't paying attention to where she is walking, she just keeps looking over the crowd, and this enables me to push the cart right in her way, so she stumbles into it.

"Oh, I'm sor..." She stops mid-word when she sees it's me. "Bitch!" she hisses, then immediately steps around the cart and throws her arms around me.

"Can you believe I'm really here?" I break away from her tight embrace. As much as I love her, I still find hugging awkward.

"I'm so happy and equally mad that you didn't prepare me."

I wave her off with my hand. "Yeah, yeah, yeah, I didn't need you riding my ass. I do things on my own time."

"Don't I know it." She rolls her eyes.

"I'm glad they gave you the day off today."

"I know how you feel about carrying your luggage through the tube," she says, laughing.

"It's not so much the luggage as your London power walk."

"Come on, let's get your stuff in the car. Are you hungry?"

"Crepes?" I grin. I can almost taste the sweet crepes we always get as soon as we hit Covent Garden. It's so surreal to think that I don't have to cram in all the food and sites with her quickly this time, because this time I won't be leaving.

"Of course, it's our place."

"Well let's crack on," I say with my best English accent and laugh.

"Oh Lord, Mary Poppins is back," she mutters and shakes her head as she starts her London power walk through the airport.

---

I wonder if the sight of London will ever get old. I take in all the buildings as we walk our way through Covent Garden to the little crêperie that is nestled in the basement of the old apple market. I find a new statue or detail on a building every time I'm here.

Although, I take pride in being a serious businesswoman, there is a young girl inside me who adores this historic place and gets lost in fantasies about a time far back in history when perhaps Kings and Queens could be seen visiting. I know it's silly, this was an old apple market, not the kind of place you'd find a royal taking a stroll, but it's nice to dream.

"How hungry are you?" Louise asks as we walk into the shop.

"I can eat, what do you have in mind?"

"I thought we could get our usual and then share one."

"Sounds perfect to me."

She orders for the both of us, and I hand cash over to the woman behind the counter.

"Are we starting this already?" She rolls her eyes and grabs our drinks.

"Does it ever actually end?" I take my change.

We take a seat by the front window so we can people watch outside. I'm silent as I look at the people running about their day.

"You are so funny." Louise puts my lemon drop crêpe down in front of me.

"I know but what did I do this time?"

"You look around with wonder in your eyes and a silly grin on your face." She cuts into her crepe, putting a bite into her mouth and closes her eyes moaning.

"It's different this time though. I don't ever *have* to leave."

"I know, I can't believe it. I always thought it was a far-fetched dream."

I flash her a look that tells her I always knew I would get here, even if she didn't believe it. Then I take a huge bite of my crêpe. The sweet and sour of the lemon and sugar tickles my taste buds and I groan. "These get better each time I have one."

We finish up and walk back to Louise's place nearby, it's really hard to believe this is now my home. I've dreamed of it for so long, that to be here finally makes all the shit I went through with Henry worth it.

"How many times has Henry called you?" Louise asks with perfect timing as always.

"He can't." Laughter bubbles up inside me and I giggle loudly.

"What do you mean he can't?" She frowns.

"I gave back my work phone and laptop before I quit and I've had all the mail and voice mails forwarded to him."

"So if he emails or calls you?"

"It goes right back to him." We stop at the door to her building and lean into each other laughing.

"Oh my God, Charlotte. That is brilliant."

"I thought so." I was pretty proud of myself. "I'll be getting a UK number tomorrow for my personal phone and never looking back."

When we reach the top of the stairs that lead to her flat, she takes her key out and unlocks the door. As soon as we step inside, a feminine voice calls out. "Lou?"

Louise looks at me and opens her mouth to tell me something, when this tiny thing races toward us up the hallway and throws herself into Louise's arms.

"I'm here! I packed my crap up and I'm all yours." She showers her face with kisses, oblivious to my presence.

"You should have called me, Cami," Louise says as she separates herself from the girl's embrace, but she doesn't seem annoyed that she is here, giving her a warm smile as she looks at her.

"I know, but I knew you wouldn't mind. I couldn't wait to be with you now that I'm free of him."

Louise kisses her tenderly. "How did it go?" she asks softly.

The girl rolls her eyes. "As we thought. But it doesn't matter now. He didn't want to share me so it's his loss." She grins at Louise. "It's just you and me, together now for real."

Louise beams from ear to ear and holds her tight.

I watch the private interaction, stunned. I don't know what to do to insert myself into the situation without it being awkward. I feel like I shouldn't be here. I close the front door behind me, the loud click bringing their attention to me.

"Who's she?" The frown that appears on the girl's face as she eyes me with suspicion is hilarious.

"Cam, this is Charlotte," Louise says, then looks at me. "Charlotte, meet..." She looks back at her with a big stupid grin. "This is my girlfriend, Cami."

I don't even have time to react before Cami rushes me and throws her arms around me. "American Charlotte? You're here! Oh my God, Lou misses you so much. I'm so glad you're here," she fires off, while squeezing me harder.

My eyes pop open, and I look to Louise for help.

"Sweetheart, let go. Charlotte doesn't do hugs." Amusement is clear in Louise's voice.

"Oh, sorry," she chirps cheerfully and steps back. "I've heard so much about you. How long are you here for?"

"Ummm, I..." I'm at a loss for words. Louise has some major explaining to do. I have never heard of this girlfriend or even gotten the impression she's had a hookup recently. She is extraordinary at keeping her little secrets then taking me to task when I do the same. I raise a questioning brow at her.

"She's come here to live, Cami," Louise answers for me, ignoring my accusing stare. "I just found out a couple of days ago." She still has the nerve to frown at me for keeping my secret when here we are right in the freaking middle of hers.

"Brilliant!" Cami exclaims. "The three of us are going to have so much fun living together." She gives me another quick hug.

I raise my brow at Louise and mouth, 'Girlfriend?' over Cami's shoulder. Louise just shrugs her shoulders and smirks.

"Oh sorry, no hugging." Cami suddenly remembers and releases me, stepping back to stand at Louise's side, taking her hand and linking their fingers together.

"It's okay, baby." Louise laughs. "She'll get over it."

Baby? Good Lord, she is going to have to do some serious talking.

"Good." Cami giggles. "I mean how can you not like hugging? Is that an American thing?" she asks in her sing-song voice. I can already tell Cami is a person with no social filter whatsoever.

"No, they hug in America," I inform her. "This is a 'Charlotte' thing," I say as gently as I can, looking over her shoulder at Louise who is shaking her head.

"Did you just refer to yourself in the third person?" Cami asks with a confused look on her face.

"Yes."

"Oh!" She looks back at Louise and snorts. "She's funny."

Louise rolls her eyes. "She is, but don't tell her that, she gets a big head."

"I am," I agree, still chuckling.

Cami's eyes light up and she claps her hands excitedly. "We need to celebrate tonight."

"I have a job interview tomorrow," I tell her, trying to dampen the flames before they get out of control. She's a live wire and I'm not sure I can handle her kind of celebration when I have important things to take care of.

"What time?" Cami cocks her head to the side.

"Two P.M.," I sigh, knowing I've just sealed my own fate.

"Plenty of time to have a few hours out on the town. I can get us on the guest list at The Roof Gardens." She looks over at Louise pleadingly.

Louise is in, I can tell from her expression. "What do you think, Charlotte? That's the club you've been dying to go to." She puts her arm around Cami and pulls her in to her side.

"I suppose a night out won't hurt. Do you mind if I take a little nap first?" The pictures of the club online flash through my head and I wonder if I will be able to sleep at all.

Louise narrows her eyes slightly. "You know that you should just push through and go to bed tonight."

"Yeah I know, but I haven't been sleeping well this last week. On the plane over, instead of going to sleep I watched three movies. I can't even remember the last time I watched one movie, let alone three." I run a hand through my hair, tiredness evident as I slump my shoulders slightly.

"Okay, I think we can let you have a short nap then."

"Thanks." I roll my eyes. "It was a pleasure to meet you, Cami." I smile weakly through the awkwardness and head straight down the hallway to the guest bedroom where we already left my luggage before our mandatory crêpe date.

Stepping into the bedroom, I close the door behind me and sigh. I sounded so formal just then. I have to remember that I am in a social setting not a boardroom, something I find difficult at the best of times, but when I'm floored with so much new information, it's hard not to click into my default state.

The walls are thin and they are still just on the other side of the door, so I hear it clearly when Cami whispers to Louise, "Did she know you were into girls?"

"She knows how I feel, love has no gender," Louise murmurs and they both go silent.

Kissing no doubt.

# FOUR

Gin and tonic always tastes better in London, I think it's like New York and its pizza. There is just something in the water that makes things taste better where they were meant to be served.

The pictures online don't do The Roof Gardens justice, next time we should have dinner here before we go dancing.

Cami has a lot of friends here, they are all casually hanging out around the sofas. She's wearing a little sparkly skirt and a halter top, super femme and the exact opposite of Louise. Louise always moves to the beat of her own drum and today she is wearing a pinstriped tailored suit that complements her curves.

I stand off to the side, listening to all the chatter but not joining in the conversation. I am just relaxing, happy to take in my surroundings and observe. I make eye contact with Louise who has Cami sitting in her lap and raise my glass in salute.

The DJ is playing some great dance tunes and I'm almost at the point where I will go dance. I've never been a woman of many words. I like to have meaningful conversations rather than trivial small talk, but when it comes to dancing I can really let go.

"Do you dance, Charlotte?" Cami asks. I tear my eyes off the dance floor and she gives me a knowing look. Apparently we have this in common.

"I love to dance," I shout over the loud bass of the song that's just started to play.

Louise slips her hand into Cami's and smiles. "Do you want to?"

"Yes!" Cami yells, fist pumping into the air. She leaps up off of Louise's lap and steps aside for her to stand up.

She's high energy, I laugh to myself. I don't know how long I could keep up with her. Louise grabs her hand and starts to pull her onto the dance floor, Cami quickly turns to grab my free hand pulling me with them.

Louise gives me a smirk then winks when she steps closer to Cami and starts grinding on her. Laughter I can't control erupts, I can't remember the last time I've felt this way. I'm free. No worries about what Henry is going to do next or what will happen to all the employees he might screw over. It feels good, it feels damn good.

I close my eyes and just move to the beat of the music, taking a second here and there to sip my drink. One song turns into the next and when I finally open my eyes the dance floor is packed and my drink is empty. I hold it up in the air and it's quickly taken out of my hand.

The music is pumping and a positive vibe fills the air around the packed dance floor. Louise and Cami are still close, as are a few of their friends, but I'm happy with my own company, lost in the music. The smile hasn't left my face since I got here. I think I'm going to like the carefree me that lives in London. Suddenly, I get bumped from behind then grabbed tightly by my upper arms, before I fall into the person in front of me.

"Pardon me," a voice says loudly close to my ear to be heard over the beat.

I shiver as a warm breath hits the sensitive spot below my ear.

The voice sounds oddly familiar. I pride myself on being great with names, faces and recognizing voices, but I don't know anyone here but Louise, and now Cami so how...?

I turn around to see and meet a pair of familiar blue eyes, which widen with surprise, before he schools his features.

"Hi...uh..." I pause, trying to remember his name, then it dawns on me that I didn't get it earlier today.

Still holding me by my upper arms, a slow smile spreads across his face, quite at odds with the pounding rhythm surrounding us. He leans in closer so I can hear him over the music. "What's your name, kitten?"

I pull back to look at him, laughing at the name. I suppose there are much worse names to be called, but I've never been a nickname sort of person. No one has ever called me anything other than Charlotte and I prefer to use people's full names.

I move closer and shout my response. "Charlotte. What's yours?"

He holds up a finger, motioning for one moment, then takes my hand in his and walks off the dance floor. We walk out onto the open air patio area and I notice out of the corner of my eye Louise and Cami are right alongside us. Close enough to help me if I need them, but far enough away that they won't be able to hear our conversation.

I ignore them for now and focus my attention on the tall dark semi-stranger before me. "Forgive me, I didn't get your name this morning."

He chuckles deeply. "No, you didn't give me a chance. I'm Rhys."

"It's a pleasure to meet you, Rhys." I hold my hand out to shake his. He looks at it for a moment, then takes it in his, lifting it up to his lips and kissing my knuckles.

I gasp. I can feel my face heating up, god damn it. Real

smooth, Charlotte, blushing for nothing. Somehow he knows how to take me out of my comfort zone, and not in a bad way.

He smiles, his lips still lingering over my skin, then he sets my hand down. I rub my finger across my knuckles, where his lips just were and swallow hard.

"Friends of yours?" His eyes continue to bore into mine, he doesn't look over to Louise and Cami once. It makes me wonder how he even knows they are there.

"Yes, my best friend in fact," I confess. It's funny to me that they think they have to stick around and watch. But I'm grateful at the same time. I've always had to fend for myself, even in my marriage. It's nice knowing Louise has my back, even if it does leave me looking like I need their protection.

"It's good that they're protective of you, this can be a dangerous city for a woman on her own," he says softly.

"Who says I'm a woman on my own?" I challenge.

Rhys gives me a knowing look. "You were traveling alone today and your friend met you at the airport. You're here with friends tonight. I think it's a fair assumption."

I nod once, conceding the point, but not offering him any actual information.

"If you were mine, you wouldn't be spending your first night in London out with friends." His eyes seem to darken as he speaks and I feel my face flush again.

I'm used to being in control, leading conversations the way I want them to go. I don't know how to deal with the way this man seems to put me off balance or why I'm not opposed to it.

"Rhys darling." A blonde woman steps up beside him, looking me up and down, then turns to him.

"Lisa." His jaw firms slightly and he has regret in his eyes.

It doesn't take a rocket scientist to know they are here together. She steps even closer to him putting her arm around his waist, his stance becoming even more rigid. She towers over me with her reedy thin frame and bleached blonde hair. Her makeup is perfect, flawless...well that's until you get to her eyebrows. Those are painted on thick and dark. I inwardly grimace at how harsh the look is, making a mental note to ask Louise if that is a 'thing' here.

"Who's your little friend?" She turns, giving me an up and down look again.

I stand a little taller, it irritates me when women act like this. "I'm Charlotte," I inform her on his behalf.

"Oh." She cocks her head and wrinkles her nose. I notice that nothing else on her face wrinkles and wonder how often she gets her Botox fix. "An American," she sneers.

"Don't be rude." Rhys frowns.

She playfully swats him on the chest. "Oh Rhys, she's American, rudeness is a way of life for them. Just look at their President."

I let out an affronted laugh. I open my mouth to tell this high society moron that rudeness is in fact an international language and that our President does not represent me or the vast majority of Americans. But before I can get a word out he cuts in.

"Lisa you're being impertinent. You can't base your opinion of a nation on one ridiculous person. I think you owe Charlotte an apology." He gives her a glare.

"It's quite alright, Rhys." People like her are ignorant and there is no reasoning with them. I find not acknowledging their behavior is the best solution. But hello! Mr. Scottish Laird has a vocabulary on him, he really is quite a surprise under all that ink and hair.

"No, it's not alright. Lisa, do you have something to say to Charlotte?" He quirks a brow at her.

She looks me up and down again with a sneer. "Nice outfit," she scoffs.

Wow. I have to suppress a laugh.

"Okay, we're done for the evening," he tells her, his tone cold and hard. He turns away from her toward me.

"Rhys!" she shrieks, stomping her foot like an infant. "You're not serious right now." She is so shrill, that even over the music pumping from inside, she makes my eardrums ache.

"Go home, Lisa," he dismisses her.

I cross my arms in front of me, watching the exchange, trying to figure out if Lisa is going to burst into a ball of tears like a child or start screaming like an old fish wife. His eyes narrow further and the color drains from her face.

"You're just going to let me leave alone?" She pouts, trying to play the guilt game.

He pulls out his cell phone and starts typing away. After a brief pause, he looks up at her. "Jack is downstairs waiting for you, he will see you home, then come back for me."

"You're serious, aren't you?" She has a stunned look on her face.

"Deadly," he retorts. There is no emotion there, he is the epitome of control.

I see her swallow hard, then she looks from me back to Rhys and seems to know she's fighting a losing battle. She changes tack completely and becomes contrite, nodding solemnly.

"Will you call me later?" she asks quietly. It's clear she has mastered all the ways to get what she needs in life, but she has hit a wall with Rhys tonight and is clearly shocked by the fact.

"I will talk to you tomorrow," he tells her firmly. One thing is clear from his tone, it's not going to be a pleasant conversation.

She looks up at him pleadingly. I almost feel sorry for her. Rhys is being hard on her, but whatever this is, it feels like it was a long time coming. She obviously brought it on herself. People watching is one of my favorite pastimes, I could study this exchange all night, but Lisa turns her attention to me at that moment and opens her mouth to say goodness only knows what. Then she changes her mind and closes it again.

"It was a pleasure meeting you." I can't resist twisting the knife.

Her eyes flash with anger, but she reins it in, turning away without another word and disappearing quickly through the thick crowd.

"I'm sorry," Rhys says beside me, sounding deflated.

Looking back at him, I study his face for a moment before I answer. "You don't need to apologize."

"She isn't a bad person," he assures me, though I wonder if perhaps he is trying to remind himself. "Just misguided sometimes."

"It's water under the bridge. She was just playing her girl-friend card." I look over his shoulder to see Louise fanning her face dramatically. I shake my head. If it wasn't for Cami, I would introduce them.

"It's not really hers to play," he murmurs resentfully.

"Perhaps you should tell her that."

His chuckle falls flat. I don't know why anyone would put up with behavior like Lisa's, but it's his choice. "I better get back to my friends," I tell him, feeling the need to separate myself from the beautiful man with the complicated love life.

"Can I get your number?" he asks, catching my elbow to halt me and then letting it go just as fast.

I still for a moment then look back and shake my head. "I don't think that's a good idea."

He faintly tilts his head and studies me for a moment. The crystal blue of his eyes bore into me, breaking his stare I look over at Louise and Cami.

"Charlotte," he implores in his rich whiskey voice. I move my gaze back to him, shaking my head. "How long are you in town for?"

"I'm here to stay," I reply softly.

A hint of a smile quirks on his lips. "Maybe we will run into each other again then."

"Perhaps," I offer. "If we are meant to be friends, I'm sure the stars will align and we will meet again." I was channeling my inner Louise with that line of rubbish. I have to bite the inside of my lower lip to keep myself from smiling.

"You are very intriguing, Charlotte."

My name on his lips gives me pause, but I force myself to finish our goodbye. It's for the best. This is the first day of my exciting new life, the last thing I want or need is to get tangled up in a messy break up. "I'll catch you later," I say with finality. Turning to walk away, I try to make a smooth departure but trip on air. One second I'm falling and the next I'm caught around my waist and lifted back up to my feet. I don't even have a second to process what happened before he speaks.

"Careful, kitten," he murmurs close to my ear. "You'll hurt yourself."

I shiver, goose bumps ripple down my arms. I turn around to look at him and our faces are too close for comfort. I take a step back so that I can breathe. "Thank you, I'm not usually so clumsy."

"It was my pleasure...What's your last name?"

I wonder for a moment if I want to give him that information, but then it comes unbidden from my lips. "Rose."

"Charlotte Rose." He takes my hand, bending down to kiss my knuckles. "Until we meet again," he says softly, and then he turns and walks away.

Standing there watching the way the crowd parts for him, I really see him as a Scottish Laird walking about his castle, his people parting like the ocean waters. I shake myself, what the fuck, Charlotte? I really need to stop reading my dirty little historical romances when I'm alone.

"How do you know him?" Cami asks in wonder.

Startled out of my daze, I look to my side to find both Louise and Cami standing next to me.

"Yeah, how?" Louise has her eyes narrowed and a calculating look on her face.

"I met him this morning at the airport." I look at Cami. "When Louise was late."

Louise groans and that only makes my smile wider. I won't be letting her live that down anytime soon.

Cami lets out a dreamy little sigh, staring longingly where Rhys disappeared.

Louise raises a brow then breaks out laughing, shaking her head. "Someone has a crush."

Cami blinks then throws her arms around Louise. "You know I love you, baby."

"I'm not jealous. I think it's cute." Louise kisses the tip of her nose. "Besides, he's gorgeous, I don't blame you at all."

"He asked me for my number," I confess.

Cami's eyes go wide. "Shut up! That's not like him. He's usually so elusive."

"You know him?" My gaze snap to hers, shocked.

"Our families go way back," she says flippantly. "We tend to run into each other at social functions in London and in Scotland."

"Old money," Louise stage whispers and Cami nudges her.

"Money, schmoney." Cami chuckles.

"Is he a good guy?" I can't help but ask, tucking my hair behind my ears, a nervous habit I have.

"He's perfect, that Lisa is a nasty witch though."

"She has room for improvement," I agree. "What's the story there?"

"Oh, you know, on again, off again. She has her sights on the family money. He knows he can do better, but he works hard and she's always around...true romance," she explains.

"I didn't give it to him," I tell them quickly, not wanting them to think I would knowingly come between a couple. I place a hand over my eyes shaking my head. I've been here all of ten minutes. How in the world am I even having this type of conversation already?

Louise laughs and after a couple of seconds she snorts heartily. "Oh, Charlotte! You do know how to pick them. He isn't really your type anyway."

"Yeah, I know, he has a girlfriend," I huff not mentioning his beard or tattoos.

"Eh." Shrugs Cami. "Girlfriend is a strong word for what she is. They were on the rocks since day one and now...well, I don't think there is a term for what they are I can use in polite society."

"Fuck buddies, huh?" Louise's eyes are sparkling with hysterics.

"Well, whatever they are, I won't be the reason they cease." I nod firmly.

Louise finally calms down. "Cami, do you think he has taken a fancy to Charlotte?"

"He certainly looked smitten. My guess is we haven't seen the last of him."

"I didn't come here to find a man. He is more your type, Louise." I shake my head.

They both look at each other and crack up.

"I'm sorry, Cami," I blurt, flustered. "I didn't mean offense." Ugh! I'm just getting myself in deeper and Louise is in hysterics again.

"None taken. He is totally our type." She wiggles her eyebrows up and down.

"Okay." I grimace. "I don't need a freaky visual. I just mean I don't need a boyfriend."

"We weren't looking for one either." Louise looks at Cami with a soft smile.

They are cute together. I've never seen Louise in a real relationship before, she's usually single or in something casual when I visit. All this sweetness is new to me.

"Nope, we already have a man to share," Cami chirps and then covers her mouth as she giggles.

My eyes widen. "Louise, you've been holding out on me."

She smirks and shrugs her shoulder. "You've been stressed. I didn't want to bother you."

I roll my eyes. "Bullshit. You didn't want to explain it to me or have me asking questions."

"That's not true!"

"Mmhmm, you have a lot of talking to do!"

She huffs defiantly but grins all the same. "Shall we get out of here then?" she suggests.

"Sounds good. I need to use the restroom first." I look around for a sign that indicates where they are.

"They are down that hall." Cami points to the hallway just inside the door behind me. "Do you want us to come with you?"

"No, stay here, baby." Louise pulls her into a hug and buries her face into Cami's hair. "Charlotte likes to be alone in the loo." She smirks my way.

I roll my eyes. They are a little too lovey dovey for me. "I'll be back."

Walking into the bathroom, I find that all the stalls are taken but thankfully I'm the first in line. One of the stall doors opens and I come face to chest with a sniffing Lisa. I inwardly groan, guess she didn't leave like she was told. The damn woman is an amazon. I take a step back looking up into her condescending smirk.

"Fancy that. It's the little American," she sneers.

"Excuse me." I move to the side so she can pass me. She follows so she's still standing in front of me.

"Don't think you will *ever* get between Rhys and I."

I hold up my hands. "That's the last thing I want. I'm not after your man."

"Good because you aren't refined enough for him."

"Sweetheart, he isn't even my type." Ugh, as soon as I say it I regret engaging with her.

"Darling, he is everyone's type. Everyone with any taste that is. Maybe you should just go back to 'Merica," she says with a fake accent.

My jaw tightens. "I'm a grown woman. I won't sling insults like an ignorant child." I move past her.

She curses something vicious under her breath that I miss, but I don't really care what she thinks of me.

I pause at the stall entrance and turn around to glance at her. "You might want to wipe your nose. Unless you want to advertise to everyone what you were doing in the bathroom."

Her eyes go wide, her hands flying to her face as she rushes over to the sink turning the water on. I smirk to myself closing the stall. She slams the door as she leaves the bathroom and I finish up as quickly as possible. This evening has had a little too much excitement for my taste.

As I'm washing my hands, the bathroom door bursts open and Louise's eyes snap to mine.

"Everything okay?" I quirk a brow.

"Cami just saw that Lisa woman storm out of here. I wanted to make sure you were okay."

"Aww. Were you going to be my knight in shining armor?"

"Bitch," she hisses.

"Always." I laugh. "I think I'm ready to go home now."

# FIVE

I wanted my transition to life in London to be as smooth and quick as possible and part of that is being self-sufficient and not relying on Louise for everything, which is how I find myself on day two of my new life, navigating the busy underground, alone. I've used the network plenty of times with Louise, but I'm nevertheless proud of myself for getting here unaided, and because I was extra, extra careful with my timings, I have almost an hour before my interview. Maybe I'll take in some of the sights before my meeting.

Knowing that St. Paul's Cathedral is in this neighborhood, I stop outside the tube station and take in my surroundings. I'm taken aback when I see the vast building looming only feet away down a narrow side street. I expected it to be stood in sprawling grounds, but instead find it like everything else in this city, tightly surrounded by the hustle and bustle.

Turning the corner, the cathedral rises into the sky before me. I'm in awe as I shield my eyes from the sun and take in the vast domed roof. Edward would love this building, I think to myself.

In fact, I know he would love it all as much as I do if I'm

honest and I realize my friend is perhaps the only thing I will miss from home. Deciding to share it with him, I blindly dig into my purse grabbing my phone and snap a picture.

**Me:** Miss you. - I attach the picture and hit send.

Almost immediately I get a reply.

**Edward:** Miss you too. When is your interview?

**Me:** About forty-five minutes.

I frown then, not recalling having even told him about the interview. Everything was such a whirlwind in the few days before I left, maybe I just can't remember. I must have since he knows.

**Edward:** You've got it in the bag.

**Me:** We'll see.

I'm grateful for the faith he has in me, but it raises my nerve levels. Attempting to stay calm, I begin to walk around the cathedral, taking in the facade. As much as I'd love to see inside, I don't think I should right now. I don't have enough time to fully enjoy it and I need to stay focused on the interview. I need this to go well, not for my security. I have the money to kick back and enjoy life. But free time and I are not good bedfellows. I need challenge. I need work. I need this job for my sanity.

I make my way through the gates to the churchyard and in the dappled shade I pass ancient tombs and sculptures. A bench opens up as I reach the rear of the building and I take a seat in the sunshine. It's an absolutely perfect place for me to sit and go over my presentation. I'm confident, but there is always that little twinge of doubt that creeps around in my head. I just have to keep reminding myself that they sought me out.

"Do you mind if I share your bench?" a familiar voice asks.

Looking up, the sun blinds me until he steps in front of it, shielding me from its intense light. I stop squinting as soon as I see his face.

"Rhys?" I ask, surprise evident in my voice.

He chuckles. "It is I."

"How did you find me?"

His eyes are piercing, a girl could get lost in those pretty blues.

"I work around here. It was simply luck I spotted you as I was passing." He sits down next to me.

I wonder if he works at a local tattoo shop or something. He's wearing ripped jeans and an old band t-shirt in such an effortless way, he looks like he could fit in easily somewhere like that.

"You have to admit it's creepy how we keep running into each other." I frown.

"Or the stars are aligned in our favor." He smirks, using my words from last night against me.

I giggle, but he doesn't look to be making a joke. "Uh huh, sure."

A slow smirk appears on his face after a beat. "Are you not a believer in fate, Mrs. Rose?"

I'm surprised at the thrill that goes through me as my name rolls off his tongue and I don't miss the direct attempt to coax my marital status out of me once again. "It's *Ms.* Rose," I inform him, throwing him a bone. "But please, call me Charlotte."

"You didn't answer the question, Charlotte." His brow raises and he waits for me to answer him.

The way my name sounds in his accent gives me goose bumps, but I force myself to snap out of my daze. "No, I don't believe in fate. I think hard work pays off and the rest will come with it."

"Ahh a cynic," he muses. "Are you staying around here?"

Interesting change of subject. "No, I'm living with my best friend Louise right now, near Covent Garden." Why am I telling him this? I'll admit he doesn't feel like a stranger, but still I'm usually not so forthcoming.

"What brings you here then? The church?" He motions over to the cathedral.

"No, I have an interview." There you go again, Charlotte! Button up your mouth. Flustered, I look at my watch. I don't do flustered. I need to get out of here. If I leave now I'll be obscenely early, but I can live with that. "In fact, I better get going." I jump up from the bench like a scalded cat.

"Would you like to meet later for coffee?" he asks hopefully.

"Sorry, Rhys, I have plans." I start to walk away and his voice travels with me.

"Until we meet again then." It's a promise, not a wish, and it stirs an army of butterflies inside me.

Shaking my head, I walk away, crossing the courtyard at a brisk pace. As I head back toward the street I came from I begin to regret my haste. Coffee wouldn't hurt. I can be friends with someone and just talk over coffee, right? I pause, giving myself a pep talk. *You can be friends with Rhys, he seems harmless.* Raising my chin higher, I turn back to Rhys, then stop in my tracks.

I watch as a familiar reedy form approaches him. He stands to greet her and she slips her arms around his waist and while I don't know him at all, I can read his body language from all the way over here. He tenses and firmly takes her forearms away from his sides, setting her back a step and looking down into her face with an expression of regret. I'm too far away to hear what they're saying. If I'm honest with myself, I don't want to know. Some things aren't worth the baggage they bring, there will always be time to make new friends later.

I turn on my heel, re-focusing on the task at hand and shaking all thoughts of a cozy coffee with a Scottish Laird away. I look at the street sign and know from my exhaustive preparations that I only need to follow this street down and around to Old Bailey. The brisk walk doesn't take much time at all and before I know it, I'm looking up at what I hope will be my new workplace.

Rhys and Lisa vanish from my mind the minute I step foot into the building. The company has been trying for the last three years to get me to interview for their Chief Financial Officer position. As soon as it became known that Henry was trying to buy me out, the offers began to pour in. Some attractive offers I have to admit, but none like this one. None that would bring me to the place I'd dreamed of living since I was a small girl. This company was the only one I considered.

I did my homework, but I couldn't find much on company policies, or a day in the life of a coworker, or who the owner even is. Whoever runs this company does a great job of keeping their name separated from the company. I can appreciate that, having spent the last decade with my name at the center of a large corporation, I know there are heady pros and heavy cons to that life. I was so proud of my baby when we started, of course I wanted to mark it as mine, but I can see the appeal of a more reclusive path and I respect anyone who chooses to take it to the top.

I straighten my jacket, stiffen my spine and hold my head up high as I walk through the door to the office and go directly to the reception desk.

The young lady has a warm, but schooled smile on her face as she recites the required greeting. "Welcome to Liberty. Can I help you?"

"Yes, I have an interview at two."

She looks down at her computer screen then back up to me and smiles once more. "Ms. Rose?"

"Yes, that's me." My voice is a lot calmer than I feel. The ultra modern interior of the reception area promises a work setting which is completely foreign to me. The Cole Financial offices were modern, yet homely. Here I feel hyper-aware of myself against the cool, sleek decor.

She nods in confirmation, typing rapidly.

"I'm sorry, I'm early," I apologize feebly and curse myself for sounding anything other than confident.

"That's quite alright, Ms. Rose. If you'll have a seat someone will be right out to take you in." She motions to the line of modern sofas in the lobby.

"Thank you." I give her a tight smile and walk over to take a seat.

As confident as I am in my ability to get this position, I feel like a fish out of water. I have been the head of a large corporation for most of my adult life, I'm not used to feeling like the shaky hopeful. There is still a chance I could blow it, simply with my lack of interview experience alone, or because I'm used to being at the top of the boardroom table, not the bottom. I've seen it when interviewing employees time and time again, candidates come in too cocky and I fear that could blow it for me. My name is well respected in the financial industry in America, but that chapter is closed. Getting into this company will start me on a new path to my career in the U.K. To achieve that I know I have to start at the bottom.

The company hit the market just like mine, I sigh and correct myself. Cole Financial is not mine anymore. I visualize the numbers I researched and repeat them in my head. I'm prepared, I'm more than qualified, I just need to interview well.

"Ms. Rose?"

I look up at the gentleman standing in the reception waiting for me and plaster a friendly smile on my face. Game on, Charlotte.

"Yes." I get to my feet carefully and walk toward him.

He puts a hand out and shakes mine firmly. I'm quietly impressed, men tend to give me weak handshakes because I'm a woman and that immediately makes me lose respect. His grip makes me feel he respects me and that we are on equal ground.

"It's a pleasure to finally meet you," he says with a

surprising amount of enthusiasm. "Come this way to the conference room." He motions me through the frosted glass doors. Pausing inside the door, I let him take the lead. In his enthusiasm I notice he hasn't given me his name. I don't want to assume he's the owner and look like I haven't done my research, but I dislike not addressing people by their name, it feels unprofessional. Entering the conference room he motions me to take a seat.

"I'm John Tesi," he tells me, allaying my concerns. "We've been exchanging emails." He pulls out a chair for me and then walks around the table and takes the seat across from me.

"It's a pleasure to put a face to the name."

"Likewise. I'm happy we were finally able to get you here for a meeting. Unfortunately, Mr. McAllister had a last minute emergency."

Inwardly I groan, I was mentally prepared to interview today and get moving on the work scene before I get too comfortable staying at home.

"Would you like to reschedule?" I offer politely, keeping my composure and not letting my disappointment show.

"No. That won't be necessary. I've prepared a packet for you. Having you come into the office was simply a formality we didn't want to bypass." He shuffles a packet of papers in front of him.

"I'm confused, John. I thought I was interviewing for the CFO position today." I frown, hoping I haven't wasted my time. I'm thoroughly confused as to why they would have a packet for me if there was no interview taking place.

He softly chuckles. "Ms. Rose, we have been watching you for a long time, we know everything we need to know about your work ethic and you come highly recommended on a personal level. Our decision has already been made. We wanted to have you come in to the office today for your formal offer."

"You don't want to ask me a series of 'tell me about a time' questions?" I almost let my mouth hang open. Mr. Tesi has thrown me completely off-guard.

"The recommendation letters we have received are more than enough. We know you'll be a great asset to Liberty, that is if you accept." He pushes a packet across the table toward me, then folds his hands in front of him expectantly.

I don't reach for the packet, I can feel my hands shaking in my lap and my heart is beating in my throat. "I accept," I blurt, with a certainty that shocks even me.

"Don't you want to review our offer?" John raises his eyebrows in surprise.

My nerves fade away. I know I'm not being hasty here. Somehow I can just feel it. They wanted me. I was the best in America and now I will be the best in England. My mouth curls into a smile and I feel an air of confidence that I can be sure isn't undue cockiness, surround me.

"Tell me, John, is this a competitive offer?"

He has schooled his features and I think there is a faint twinkle in his eye. "Ms. Rose, our offer would top any competition, I assure you. You were sorely underpaid in your last role, owner or not."

I incline my head. "I pride myself on trusting others until they prove me wrong. So I trust that this offer won't offend me and I accept the position." I stand up and reach across the table to shake his hand.

He clasps my hand firmly. "I look forward to working with you, Ms. Rose."

"Please, call me Charlotte. When would you like me to start?" I sit back down. I don't know how much longer I can contain my excitement.

"Well, we would like to begin the process as soon as possible. How long are you in town for?" He moves his notepad in front of him and picks up his pen to take notes.

"Oh, I have moved here indefinitely," I tell him, folding my hands together so I don't restlessly tap on the table. "I don't plan to return to the US."

The look of surprise on his face brings a smile to mine. "I see. Have you already found a place to stay?"

"My best friend lives here. I'll stay with her until I find an area I'd like to live in. My possessions are in storage with a shipping company until I'm settled."

He nods, scribbling a note on his pad. "If you need some suggestions, I can assist there."

"Thank you. I'll keep that in mind." I get a good vibe from John, I'm usually a good judge of character and the way he is showing interest in his employee's well-being shows he has a decent respect for the people he works with.

"We should discuss getting you a work visa then. We want to make sure everything is official. That is a top priority. We will of course sponsor you and I don't anticipate any issues."

I give him a satisfied smile as I know all my hard work and preparation for this moment is about to pay off. "That won't be necessary, John. You see, my father was British, so I have used my hereditary right to apply for citizenship. I received my British passport last week. I'm free to stay here unsponsored. If you have more information on what other documents you'll need, I'll gladly supply them for you."

John laughs. "Well, it seems you are five steps ahead of us, Charlotte. We missed that little gem in our research on you."

"I like to be prepared in advance."

"Splendid. This is going to be a fantastic partnership." He looks down at his notes and scrubs his pen over them, realizing all of the items on his to do list are already taken care of. "Well since there aren't weeks of procedure to get through, how soon would you like to start?"

"I can start as soon as you'd like."

"Right then, we are very keen to get you on board. We're going into the weekend now so what say you start fresh and clear on Monday morning? It will just give us a day or two to prepare for your arrival. Will that work for you?"

"That will be perfect. Do we start at seven am?"

"No. We start our day at eight."

"I'll be here," I confirm, trying my hardest not to bounce in my chair. A whole new challenge awaiting me after the weekend is more than I had hoped for out of today and the thought of sinking my teeth in has me bouncing with excitement. "I just want to thank you for this opportunity, John," I tell him, controlling my voice.

"Charlotte, I'll be honest, it is us who should be thanking you. The minute word went out that you would be leaving your company we knew we had to have you as part of the Liberty family. This is an excellent company to work for. I have been here since the start and every year it just gets better. I think you'll enjoy working with us."

"I believe I will. Is there anything I should prepare myself for on Monday?"

John shakes his head. "No, your first day will be introducing you to everyone. After that we can sit down and talk about our game plan and a high-level review of the finance department." He stands up, walks around the boardroom table and holds a hand out to me. Taking it, I let him help me stand.

"Sounds perfect to me, I'll see you on Monday." He walks me back to the front lobby and I pause, turning to him and smiling. "Thank you again."

"I'm glad we were able to get to you first, Charlotte. Now I hope we can do the same with Edward."

My eyes go wide. "You know Edward?"

"Edward is my cousin. He never told you?"

"That little stinker! No, he never mentioned it. No wonder he knew when I was interviewing."

"Perhaps he thought you'd prefer to know you were being headhunted for your own merits."

"Well, he was right about that," I confirm with a nod. "Are you trying to bring him over too?"

"Yes. My hope is that now that you're here, he will soon follow." He glances at his watch. "I hate to cut you short, but with Mr. McAllister out I have double appointments. I will see you on Monday."

"Have a good weekend, John."

"You too."

He goes back inside without another word. I leave the office elated and head back the same way I came. I'm sure I have a stupid grin on my face but I'm too happy to care.

When I return to Louise's flat, I find Louise at the kitchen counter making tea. She looks up and immediately I know I'm not going to like the next words out of her mouth. We have this innate ability to read each other, even when we have been apart for months.

"What is it, Louise? You have that look."

She rolls her eyes, annoyed that I can read her as well as she reads me.

"Don't get mad," she begins.

"That is never a good start to a sentence." I scowl.

"She means well..."

My eyes widen. "Cami? What did she do?"

"There's this guy she knows from work. He's really nice apparently."

I fold my arms. "Good for him, why do I need to know this information, Louise?"

She sighs. "She kind of offered to set the two of you up on a blind date."

"She—" I open my mouth and close it again. "I—but—" I pull my raging thoughts together and tell her the clearest one in my head. "Nope! No. Never going to happen. Nuh-uh. Nope." Vigorously shaking my head, I turn and head for my room, Louise hot on my heels.

"Come on, Char, you might like him. You said you wanted to start living a little."

I stop at my door. "Louise, I know what I said, but I have been in London for mere hours. I have barely unpacked my luggage. I had a job interview today - which I got by the way." I shoot her a pointed look.

"Wow, congratulations. I was just going to ask—"

"Uh huh." I cut her off by holding up my hand. "If I'm going to start living a little, I would like to do it in my own time, preferably after I have caught up on some sleep. I certainly don't need to be set up with a stranger before I've even had a chance to unpack!"

Louise bites her lip as the need to laugh at my outburst overcomes her.

Her battle causes my scowl to falter and I too have to fight a reluctant smile.

"I'll tell Cami to hold off for a while on the matchmaking," she giggles.

"You tell her what you like, I'm not going on a blind date. Period."

"Yeah, yeah. So how did it go today?"

"Really well," I tell her. "I took the job. I start Monday."

She squeals and throws her arms around me. "So this is it? You're really staying?"

I peel her off me, not especially minding the hug, but nipping it in the bud anyway. "Of course I'm staying. I told you that already."

"I know you did, but this makes it really real!"

I shake my head. "Yes, it's really, really real. I'm here for good. My new life has officially begun. And you'd better tell that girlfriend of yours I really, really won't be going on any damn blind dates. Clear?"

Louise smirks, then flings her arms around me again. "Crystal."

# SIX

The commute, even in the heat of rush hour, wasn't bad. The train was packed but I can deal with it. It's cleaner than New York, less humid, and the people are also so much more polite. Heck even a bloody hell sounds more polite than a New Yorker's hello.

There is a Costa coffee house right on my way in, so of course that is my first stop. The excitement of a new job has adrenaline buzzing through my veins, but a girl still needs her coffee. I should be a little afraid to start a new job but I'm just thrilled for the challenge. I felt so naked, so empty-handed without my work around me. Today that ends.

"Almond milk latte, please," I say to the barista as soon as he turns his attention on me. I'm ordering differently than I did stateside. Not getting the two extra shots is a change, right? I don't feel like I need them. I'm rested, refreshed, and ready to take on the world. I pay and wait in line eagerly for my drink. Once I get the paper cup in my greedy hands I can't wait. I gingerly take that first sip, careful not to burn myself, and sigh.

"That must be a good cuppa, kitten," says a now familiar and damn sexy Scottish voice beside me.

"Rhys." His name comes out as a breathy sigh. Damnit. What was that?

"You remembered my name, that's a good sign." He gives me a cocky smirk, showing his perfect white teeth and effectively snapping me out of whatever that was.

"I'm very good with names," I tell him with a knowing smile, not needing to feed his ego more than it probably is daily. I raise my free hand and count off on my fingers. "Rhys...Lisa...am I forgetting anyone?"

A full-blown belly laugh bursts out of him. "Oh, kitten has claws."

I give him a flat look. "I have to get going. Have a nice day and tell Lisa I said hello." The parting shot was totally unnecessary and all it did was make the big oaf smile wider.

He ignores my dismissal and turns to follow me out the door. "Late for an appointment?"

"Actually, it's my first day at work." Ugh! Stop telling this man your business. He's a complication I do not need in my life right now. The complication is not all him, he has baggage too. I shouldn't forget that. Why does someone as nice as him have to be attached to a nasty bint of a woman? I almost let a laugh out, catching myself using Cami's slang. If Louise heard me using that word she would never let me live it down.

"A penny for your thoughts," he asks as he follows me out of the coffee shop.

"I bet you don't even remember my name," I blurt accusingly. If it wouldn't add to my humiliation, I would clap my hand over my mouth. Sometimes my lips move faster than my brain and now I've handed him the satisfaction of knowing that I hoped he would remember it. Awesome. I stop walking outside the coffee shop. I have to shake him off before I continue so that he won't know which way I'm going when we part. It's freaky that I keep running into him everywhere and I really need to start this work day focused solely on work.

"How can one forget a name like yours?" he asks, ignoring the tone of my outburst. "It could be right out of a sonnet."

I narrow my eyes at him, noting with some satisfaction that he didn't actually use my name so he's probably just blowing hot air. "Aren't you a little word slinger."

"You're a funny woman, Charlotte Rose."

That shuts me up. He did know it, damnit. I'd assumed he was calling me kitten because he didn't remember. I imagined he had many kittens, maybe a few darlings, or sweethearts. I would have called him out on it sooner, but I've never had anyone call me a pet name before and some sappy part of me sort of likes it. God, I hate myself sometimes.

Squaring my shoulders, I decide to draw this pointless conversation to an end. "It was nice bumping into you again, Rhys, but I must get going."

"It was indeed a pleasure," he agrees then he cocks his head to the side. "Although I am starting to think you're following me. First the airport, then the bar and now twice near where I live."

This guy is so full of himself. "I was thinking the same thing about you," I retort.

"I wouldn't need to follow you around if I had your number, kitten." His confidence kills me. We both know these meetings have been purely coincidental, but he's so relaxed with himself he's happy to wear the role of would be stalker, whereas I had to deflect to save face. Ugh.

"I think that maybe we should just call this chance and go on our way. I don't think Lisa is ready for you to be friends with another woman," I tell him, attempting to get some control over the situation. I glance at my watch briefly to check that I am still as early as I planned to be. It's fine, I have plenty of time, but Rhys catches the action and takes it as a hint.

"Lisa doesn't govern who I'm friends with, but I will let you get on with your day." With a hint of reluctance, he steps back. "Until we meet again, kitten."

I stand there for a few seconds watching his retreating back, feeling like I just missed out on an opportunity. I could kick myself. I've never been afraid of what anyone thinks of me. Much less a coked-up burn-out of a woman. This has not been a great start to my day. I need to focus on what matters. I'm Charlotte Rose, successful businesswoman, winner of the Lloyds Bank National Business Award and now, CFO for Liberty. Right now, that is all that matters. I have to head in the same direction Rhys went but I'm relieved to find that he has been swallowed by the crowd ahead. I think I've had all the Rhys based excitement I can take for one morning.

When I arrive, I try to soak up the feeling of being an employee for the first time in years. It's strange, without as much responsibility, I can concentrate on my specific job and not have to worry too much about all the risk assessments and red tape. Not my responsibility anymore. I can suggest what's best for the company and how to action my suggestions. The politics are up to someone else. It's very liberating. Ironic that Liberty is the company to give me freedom, I chuckle to myself as I approach the reception desk. I don't have a security pass yet, so I need to sign in first and find out where to go. The young woman at the desk looks up with a smile. "Ms. Rose?"

"Yes, that's me." I'm impressed. They must have one awesome communication system for her to know me by sight already.

"Welcome to Liberty! I have a packet for you," she says warmly, coming around the desk to greet me. She picks up a sleek looking black leather folio and hands it over to me. I'm surprised by its weight as I take it. "The pack includes a copy of your contract, the company policies booklet, our personal brochure and your laptop and mobile phone." She remembers another item and leans over her desk to reach it. "And here is your security pass for the building."

"Goodness, thank you." I take it all from her slightly overwhelmed to be greeted with a welcome package at the door. "I'm sorry, I didn't catch your name."

"Oh! I'm sorry, Ms. Rose, my name is Lily."

"It's a pleasure to meet you, Lily. And thank you for all of this."

"Oh, no." Lily waves me off. "Mr. McAllister gets all of the new hire packets together himself. He usually likes to deliver them personally and settle you in to your office, but he had something unexpected pop up so he left it here for you, so that you weren't kept waiting."

"Charlotte, good morning." John enters the reception with a paper cup that matches mine.

"Mr. Tesi, good morning, I'm very excited to start the day," I jabber, noticing a distinctly nervy quality to my voice. First days are as bad as first dates, and I swore I'd seen the last of both. But here I am anyway, and I am nervous, but only because it's all so new. I know myself and my ability to more than do this job.

John smiles warmly, recognizing the plethora of emotions crossing my face and offering me reassurance. He trusts in my capabilities too, he really does remind me of Edward now that I know they are related. This reminds me I need to touch base with Edward to see what he's doing now and heck, if I can get him here that would be wonderful.

"Please call me John. Lily, is Mr. McAllister in his office?"

"No, I was just explaining to Ms. Rose. He popped in early and left her packet with me. He said he would try to come back later, but said if you have any problems to text him."

I've become good at reading people so I see the slight surprise register on John's face before he clears the faint expression and turns to me with a smile.

"There will be plenty of time for you to meet Mr. McAllister. Come, I'll show you around the office."

Thanking Lily again, I follow John through security, showing my brand-new pass and to the elevators, now laden down with my own bag, my coffee and the weighty folio. John presses the call button and once inside, he presses the button for the tenth floor. He looks up at me and notices me eyeing the panel, taking in the number of floors in the building and where we are headed within them.

"Executive offices are on the tenth floor," he informs me. "The ground floor is conference space and meeting rooms, eleven is our wellness center."

My brows raise.

John chuckles at my reaction. "It's okay, Charlotte, it's not for everyone. But Mr. McAllister takes the whole mind body and soul thing seriously, so Seersha is available to all employees."

"Seersha?" I ask, unsure what he means.

"That's the name of the wellness center." He continues to smile, enjoying my baffled expression. "There is a fully kitted out gym, running track, pool and sauna/steam rooms. There is a yoga studio where you can attend weekly classes or book one-on-one sessions, and there are quiet rooms if you need to decompress."

My eyes must be wide as saucers by now and John's amusement confirms it.

"Mr. McAllister wants all his employees to have the facilities to improve their overall wellness if they wish to. He believes that a happy team makes a healthy business."

My mind goes right to Henry. This is what I was always telling him, but he saw anything that didn't directly benefit him as not his problem. It was always a battle with him to provide our staff with even the basics for a positive work environment.

"It's not mandatory," he assures me. "Think of it as a perk."

"No, I think it's fabulous. I'm just a little surprised is all."

"Mr. McAllister is a surprising man on many fronts." John smiles fondly.

"Interesting," I muse.

"You'll see when you meet him."

I glance back at the display panel and watch the floors count off as we pass them.

"What about twelve through fifteen?"

"Mr. McAllister owns the entire building. The upper floors are apartments."

The elevator arrives on our floor and the doors open. "Who lives there?" I ask as we step off into a reception area.

"One or two of the executives, some are rented and Mr. McAllister has the penthouse. If you decide to start looking for a permanent place to live, we do have a vacancy. I kept it available since you said you are staying with a friend until you get settled," John tells me as we pass through the reception and into the office space.

This isn't the typical work environment I'm used to with the rows of cubicles. It's sleek and modern with low standing walls set up like a hive. Little pods with tables in-between, plenty of communal space for interaction and collaboration. I like it already.

"I might be interested," I tell him as I take it all in. "I would have to think about it. Do you live here?"

"I used to. We moved out of the city a couple of years ago to be near our grandkids."

I gasp. "You can't have grandkids, John. You're too young!"

John laughs. "Charlotte, you say all the right things. We have two, but they are both under five, so I guess you could call me a beginner grandad."

"You wear it well, that's all I'm saying."

"Good morning, Mr. Tesi," a soft spoken voice interrupts our laughter.

"Oh, Jo, I'm glad you're here. Charlotte, this is Jo Silver, she will be your executive assistant. Jo, this is Ms. Rose."

I want to reach a hand out and give Jo a firm handshake, but my hands are full. "It's a pleasure to meet you."

"Would you like me to take Ms. Rose around and show her where everything is?" Jo asks him.

"Thank you, Jo, but I am going to spend a little time with Charlotte this morning and I can show her around a little bit."

"Perfect." She smiles and reaches out her hands. "Let me take your welcome pack and put it in your office for you. Then everything will be ready for you when you're done with Mr. Tesi."

"Thank you." I hand over the folio and she takes my bag, leaving me with just my coffee which I sip as I follow John for my tour.

After a complete walkthrough of all the areas that concern me, including but not limited to the locations of the bathrooms, I find myself sitting in my spacious office, at my new desk with a huge smile on my face. I think I'm going to be happy here. I'm fully aware that today is likely to be the most relaxed day I get to experience, but I am ready for the hard work to begin.

It feels like a positive environment. The staff seem content and productive. If only Henry could see the evidence of what caring for your staff can reap for you, but I realize too late that Henry has no place in my thoughts, today or any other day for that matter. He is in the past, along with Cole Financial. My focus now is myself and Liberty.

What I did learn today is how efficient they are in the set-up of a new coworker. When I opened my folio, I found a brand-new

MacBook Pro, all set up ready for me, my new iPhone, fully charged, an information pack on the company, all my logins ready to use, and access to the reporting tools to pull financial numbers. I haven't had to ask for or wait for a thing.

Mr. McAllister does a fine job of ensuring a professional transition.

A light knock at my door draws my attention from the brochure. "Ms. Rose, it's five p.m., most of the office is leaving for the evening. Did you need help finding your way to the tube station?" Jo asks sweetly.

"Thank you, I remember the way. You have a nice evening, Jo," I tell her. "And please, call me Charlotte."

Jo smiles, a slight blush staining her cheeks. "I'll see you tomorrow, Charlotte. Have a good night."

"You too."

She quietly shuts my office door and leaves me once again alone. The silence of the office is my sign, I can't start working twelve-hour days right from the start. I'm breaking my habit, right? Yes. I decide to pack up my stuff and go home at a normal hour. Maybe I can cook Louise some dinner.

# SEVEN

I'm proud of myself. I've made it through my first two weeks at Liberty. It has been a busy couple of weeks which had me just outside my comfort zone, but it was good for me. I'm still waiting to meet the elusive Mr. McAllister, but we keep just missing each other.

I'm trying to figure out why exactly they felt they needed to hire me and offer my salary, when the company is doing as well as it is. It's profitable and organized. Sure there are a few key areas that I can improve upon, but it felt like they headhunted me to prevent a crisis of some kind and I haven't seen one yet. I want to ask, but I don't want to make myself sound redundant. I'm certain they knew what they were getting when they hired me, so I'm just going to do my job and hope I impress them.

It's the weekend, so I'm going to do what I promised myself and leave work at the office. TGIF, right? I pack up my bag, still astonished at how light it is now that I genuinely leave my work at the door. In years past I would rarely be home before nine...ten maybe, and when I was, I was laden down with files. I feel naked,

I'm not going to lie, but I'm doing my best to follow the lead of my coworkers, rather than fall into my old habits.

Louise's flat is usually empty when I return to it, but for once she's home before me.

"Hey, Louise, how was your day?" I hang my briefcase in the hall closet and join her on the sofa with a huff.

"Alright, sick of my boss' bullshit so I left on time," she replies. "How was your day?"

"Pretty good, want to order some Wagamamas, take our bras off and chill for the rest of the night?" I stretch out the tension I had left in my body and look to her expectantly. With no Cami here, we could have a really relaxed evening.

"You are obsessed with that ramen!" she scoffs.

"It's. The. Best. I could eat it every day."

"Well, you're not eating it today. We have a reservation at THE hard to get into BBQ joint in Soho. The waiting list is like three months. Cami got us in somehow. I don't know her methods, but trust me it's going to be good."

"You have to wait three months to get into a BBQ joint around here?" I ask incredulously, suppressing my groan at another night out with Cami.

"Char, this is London. BBQ joints aren't exactly sitting on every corner waiting to throw burnt ends at you every time you pass. This place is the real deal, American owned, American run. *Time Out* listed it in their top ten BBQ places in the world. Bookings are crazy and Cami had some connection. So leave your bra where it is woman because I want BBQ and you're coming."

I huff, because I had my hopes high for being braless, but BBQ does sound good.

"Earth to Charlotte." Louise snaps her fingers in front of my face.

"Yeah alright, I'll keep my bra on for good BBQ, but it had better be amazing."

"You are going to love it, I promise. Now go get changed."

I stand with a groan and head for the hall.

"And wear something sexy," she adds as I reach the doorway.

"Sexy...To a BBQ joint? What for? It's just you and Cami. Who am I trying to impress?"

"You never know who will be there, Charlotte. Be. Prepared."

"I think you have me confused with a girl scout."

"Just do it," she demands and I turn with a groan and head for my room.

A couple of hours later, I'm being ushered enthusiastically through the door of a pretty cool looking BBQ joint and I will admit, it smells like heaven. Although, why Cami and Louise are so excited, I don't know. I doubt they would know good BBQ from bad.

Cami speaks to the hostess and to my surprise despite the wall to wall people, we are taken straight through to our table, leaving many customers in the bar still waiting to be called. I must find out what Cami's connections are exactly, because this is impressive by anyone's standards.

We're led past the open pit in the center of the restaurant. Sausage links hang smoking above, their aroma filling the entire space. We pass table after table of diners with food to die for and head right for the booths in the back. They are all full except one, and I'm surprised to find that there is already someone sitting in the only one that could be ours. Cami and Louise however seem less surprised.

I smell a rat and fight the urge to run.

He's not looking our way as we approach, so I have the chance to size him up without being caught. He has softly curly rich brown hair and a neat beard with a peppering of silver. I can't see the color of his eyes, only his profile is visible to me, but his charcoal gray suit looks tailored to perfection and I find myself checking off boxes on my list. *Dark, check. Smartly dressed, check.*

As we approach the table he turns. Damn. Well isn't he a sight for sore eyes? *Handsome, check.* He stands...*Tall, check*...and smiles. Perfect, his smile is simply perfect.

Jesus. I don't know what's going on here, but it annoys me that I'm falling in line with it. *Show some self-control.*

"Cami!" he exclaims in an American accent.

"Michael." She grins from ear to ear, kissing him on the cheek. "This is Louise," she tells him, stepping aside so that he can greet Louise in the same fashion.

"It's good to finally meet you," he tells her, kissing her cheek.

"You too."

Cami cuts their introduction a little short however when she says pointedly, "And this is Charlotte."

Michael glances first at Cami before turning to me and introducing himself, and I don't miss the faint look of realization flicker across his face. "I'm Michael, pleased to meet you."

He leans in to kiss my cheek. "I think we're being set up," he whispers.

I laugh aloud, I can't help myself. "You could be right," I reply in the second before he pulls away.

Louise is looking worried. Cami looks like the cat that got the cream. I shake my head at the pair of them.

Michael smiles knowingly and motions for me to sit. I slide in to the booth and watch the scramble ensue between Louise and Cami. In the blink of an eye, Louise is beside me, preventing me from escaping the enclosed booth and Michael has been positioned opposite me, wedged in firmly by Cami. Those two are about as subtle as an elephant stampede.

"Your waiter will be with you shortly," the hostess tells us, dropping the menus on the table and leaving us to some heavy tension.

"So, Michael," Louise says in what I know to be her rehearsed, stage tone. "Cami tells me your brother owns this place."

"He does." Michael grins. "He's finally useful for something."

"Hey that hurts!"

I look up to see another fine man standing at our booth. He's a more laid-back version of his brother, but other than that they are identical. Same killer smile and tall, dark, handsomeness, but without the sharp suit and the precisely cut hair, he seems more at ease. It's apparent that they are entirely different in character, but genetically they are the same. Identical twins. Hot damn.

"The truth always does," Michael retorts. "Ladies, this is my brother, Connor."

"Hi, Connor," Cami says flirtatiously. She turns to Michael. "You didn't tell me your brother was such a dreamboat," she says with a purr.

Louise giggles.

Connor barks out a laugh. "I like her," he tells Michael, pointing the tip of his pen at Cami.

"Of course you do," Michael sighs.

"Now what can I get you ladies to drink?" Connor asks.

I catch Louise and Cami exchanging some kind of look and before I can interpret its meaning, the show begins.

"Oh shoot! You know what? Lou, we have that thing."

"Shit!" Louise gasps, her stage tone back in full glory. "How could we forget the thing?"

"I know, right?" Cami takes an exaggerated look at her watch. "You know, if we hurry, we can still make it."

"Okay." Louise jumps to her feet so fast that Connor has to step out of her way. He eyes her quizzically and exchanges a look with his brother, but I can't see Michael's response because I'm too busy staring daggers at my so-called best friend.

"I'm so sorry, you two, we have to run," Cami says as she gets up too. "But you should stay and enjoy some dinner together. No sense in eating alone when you have company."

Louise winces then throws me an 'I'm sorry, it was her idea and you can kill me later' look, before they both dash out of the restaurant like the place is on fire.

A stunned silence follows.

I turn slowly to the two men whose company I have just been abandoned in.

"Wow," Connor murmurs in astonishment.

"I called it." Michael raises his hand in victory and chuckles.

I simply bury my face in my hands "Oh my God. I. Am. So. Sorry."

This is ludicrous. What the hell just happened?

Above me I hear Connor bust out laughing and Michael smacks him as he hisses, "Dude, can't you see she's upset?"

Michael gently touches one of my hands from across the table. "Hey, you have nothing to be sorry for."

I snort uncontrollably and lift my head, laughing so hard. "Really? Apart from having the worst best friend in history, who by the way is fired as soon as I find her."

"Man, that was brutal," Connor says in disbelief, slumping into Cami's seat beside his brother, still laughing. "How do you know them?"

"Cami and I work together," Michael tells him, but his eyes stay on me, full of concern and sympathy while I just do that 'if I don't laugh, I may cry' giggle.

"How about you?" Connor asks me.

"Louise is my best friend, Cami is her girlfriend."

Connor nods in understanding.

"But I just moved here, so we only just met," I assert, not wanting them to think that Cami is someone whose behavior I regularly let slide. This is all on Louise and we will be having a discussion in the morning. "I'm so sorry you got dragged into this,

Michael. I'll just go." I make to stand and Connor jumps up to block my exit.

"No stay," he says in a tone akin to desperation. "I'll bring you both a strong drink and some great food. No sense in leaving hungry when we serve the best BBQ east of Texas, right?"

I sit back down and look from Connor to Michael. Michael looks perplexed. God, poor guy does not need this drama in his life. "Connor, let her go if she wants to, it's not fair to make her sit through dinner with a total stranger when her friends have just ditched her." He turns to me. "I'll help you find a cab." He stands and as quickly as he blocked me, Connor does a sidestep and blocks his exit.

"Bro, it's the least we can do. Sit, talk, eat." He gives his brother a look that holds so much meaning. "It might be good for you," he adds pointedly.

Michael sucks in a breath, lets it out in a long sigh and slowly lowers himself back down to the seat. He looks at me for a moment and then smiles softly. "I'm game if you are."

I chew on my lip. He seems nice. It's awkward as all hell, but at least we are both in the same situation and well—the food smells too good to walk out on right now. I'm famished. "Sure, why not?"

"Excellent, strong drinks coming up," Connor says with a sense of urgency. He seems keen for us not to have time for second thoughts. "Charlotte, right?" he asks me.

I nod.

"What's your poison?"

I think for a moment. "Do you have any ciders?" I've had one or two great hard ciders on my visits to the UK. Unlike America they have some really great fruit flavors.

"We sure do." He flips over a menu, letting me peruse the selection.

I order a pear cider and Michael orders a beer, then looking pleased, Connor leaves us alone.

"I'm sorry about him."

"Why are you sorry about him? It's Cami and Louise who need to be sorry."

"Well, he's just as keen to force me onto the dating scene as they seem to be. I feel like you're here against your will now." He shakes his head. "Jesus, who needs friends and family hey?"

"I know right?"

Michael fixes me with a stare. "If we're doing this, I think we should start over don't you?"

"Agreed. I'm Charlotte." I reach my hand across the table and he takes it shaking it lightly.

"It's a pleasure to share your company, Charlotte. I'm Michael."

All the tension from the scene that just took place seems to evaporate.

"Where are you from?" Michael starts the conversation off smoothly.

"New York, you?"

"Chicago, who would have thought I'd move all the way to London only to be fixed up with someone from the states?" He chuckles deeply and his blue eyes have a twinkle to them.

"I was thinking that exact same thing." I don't know if it's the accent or him that makes me feel at ease, but I feel relaxed in his company despite the rocky beginning to the night.

"So what brings you to England?"

"Life was—you know—I just needed a fresh start. My best friend lives here and my father was born here. I applied to claim my citizenship and I got it. So the move was pretty easy. I've only been here a few weeks, but I'm happy I finally did it. What about you?"

"My story is a little like yours I guess. I couldn't stand living in Chicago any longer and decided to try London. Connor came too, we've been here full-time for a couple of years. It's...what I needed."

There is definitely a story there, but I don't know him yet, so I don't feel like I can ask. A waitress comes over with a smile for Michael and saves me from the potentially awkward silence that would have followed him giving me such cryptic, but obviously personal information. She sets down our drinks and exchanges pleasantries with my handsome dinner companion and tells us Connor will be back to take our order.

Michael hands me the menu and leaves the other one where it is.

"I suppose you eat here a lot?" I open the menu and my stomach growls excitedly at the prospect.

"More than I probably should. It's easy, close to work and awesome. This booth is always available to employees."

"You work here?"

"I have been known to roll my sleeves up on occasion. But I'm not on the payroll, unless you count brisket as a currency."

"I'd consider it. So what's good?" My eyes are darting over the menu from one temptation to another and I need some guidance.

"Everything."

"Well, I can't very well order one of everything. Do you have a favorite?"

"Hmm..." His eyes lift up as he thinks. "We could get the family sample platter so you get to try everything. It's a lot of food but we both can take home leftovers. How does that sound?"

"Perfect." I place the menu back down on the table.

He makes eye contact with someone over my shoulder and Connor appears rapidly.

"So what can I get the two of you?" Connor asks, looking at us both in turn with interest. I don't know what he is expecting to see, but he seems satisfied that we are both still here, participating in this bizarre ambush date.

"We're going to have the family platter. Charlotte wanted to know what was good and I told her, everything."

"Damn, you two can sure eat a lot."

"We'll take the leftovers home."

Conner raises his eyebrows in surprise. I guess to him it sounded like the 'we' and the 'home' meant that we would be going home together. I want to correct him, but Michael speaks first.

"Just bring the food, asshole."

"Sure thing, brother." Conner smirks as he walks away.

"So what is it you do when you aren't pitching in here?" That suit is not made for waiting tables, that's for damn sure.

"I'm in PR."

"Oh right, that's how you know Cami."

"Yeah, we work together. I'm her manager actually."

"Oh Jesus. She sprung a blind date on her boss?"

Michael doesn't look amused. "Yep. The woman has no idea when it comes to boundaries."

"You said it." I smack my palm on the table with a laugh. "But hey, she's your friend."

"I might not go so far as to say we're friends, more like friendly co-workers. Once you're off the clock, she's not my problem."

"You're here tonight though," I point out.

"She begged me to get her a table, which isn't as easy as it sounds. So I said she could join me and she asked if she could bring friends. It all sounded so innocent."

"Lesson learned."

"You're telling me." He sips his beer. "So what about you? Are you looking for work?"

"I actually landed something as soon as I arrived. I'm the new CFO for Liberty. It's a tech company."

"A woman in high demand," Michael says flirtatiously.

"Something like that." I blush.

"And how are you enjoying it so far?"

"I'm loving it, it's...well, I'm still finding my feet I guess, but a new challenge is always exciting right?"

"You don't sound so sure."

"I really like the company. It's well run and it's seems to be a positive work environment, which was important to me. I guess..." While I'm trying to finally put my concerns into actual words, our food arrives. "Holy crap, Michael, we won't be able to finish all this."

"Nope, but we're sure gonna have fun trying. Now dig in and then tell me what's bugging you about your new job."

I watch him serve himself slices of brisket and sausage, taken aback that I'm thinking of discussing my work concerns with a someone I've known an hour when I really haven't even thought to talk to Louise about it yet. But he does seem like he's interested and it would be nice to hear an impartial opinion.

"Are you going to leave me to eat all this?"

"Mmm?" I realize I was lost in thought. "Sorry, no. I was just thinking about work. You're right." I pick some food from the platter for my plate. "I'm just wondering why they need me is all. I mean, I'm kind of at the top of my game, and they knew that when they headhunted me. Until just a couple of weeks ago, I owned one of the most successful financial consultancies in the US. I guess I'm just confused because Liberty is running like clockwork. Obviously I'm still working my way through familiar-izing myself with every system and checking into all aspects of their finances, but so far, I'm not seeing why they would work so hard at bringing someone like me in when they were handling things fine."

"Maybe they want someone to come in and change things?"

"Of course, I will make some changes where I think they will fit, but if it ain't broke..." I shrug. I think it was playing on my mind more than I allowed myself to realize.

"I'm sure that the reason will reveal itself in good time. You should just focus on dazzling them with your professionalism until it does and then you'll be in a position to implement the changes they need with their trust fully in you."

I nod. "I suppose you're right. I have to stop thinking above my pay grade. I've come from owning my own company and everything that entails, to being an employee where I feel like I might be more help than they're looking for. I need to take off my CEO hat and try to think like an employee. It's something I need to work on."

"You'll get there," Michael assures me. There is warmth in his eyes when I look up. I'm glad I stayed.

Conversation flowed, well, small talk really, until our meal was over and we asked for the check.

"I've had a lovely evening, Charlotte. Thank you."

"I have too. But let's not tell Cami shall we? We can't have her thinking this was a victory, she'll be unstoppable." I laugh.

"Even more unstoppable you mean?"

"Right."

The waitress places the check on our table and Michael moves faster than I manage to.

"We can split it," I quickly insist.

"Oh no we will not." His voice is stern.

I raise a brow at him. "Do you have an issue with me paying for my own dinner?"

He runs his fingers through his hair. "Sorry, that came out

more forcefully than I meant it to. Really, it's my treat, Charlotte. Please?"

I study him. I enjoyed his company and I think I'd like to see him again, so I offer a compromise. "How about I let you get this one and the next is on me?"

"That sounds like a second date," he beams.

"It sure does."

# EIGHT

"John, something isn't adding up." I have my phone on speaker, sitting back in my office chair. I know John is in his car between meetings but I didn't want to sit on this a moment longer than necessary. Having finally got around to staff expenses, the 'something' I had been waiting for has at last shown itself. I mean, I wasn't looking for it specifically, but there is definitely something not right in the expense system.

"Give it to me, Charlotte. What have you found?"

"You say that like you were expecting me to find something." I pause and then a little paranoid voice in my head whispers an idea I wish I could unhear. "Am I being tested?" I snap.

"Not at all," John says calmly. "But I'm not shocked that you've come across something beneath the surface, let's put it that way."

"What is that supposed to mean, John? If you suspected there was an issue, you should have told me from the get-go. I can only do my job to the standard you expect if I have all the information."

"Charlotte, calm down. It's not like you think. I personally suspected something was amiss. A gut feeling. It was merely a theory, not something we hired you to find."

"Then why did you hire me?" My exasperation at the whole situation is finally too much to keep locked inside.

"Isn't that obvious?"

I don't offer any indication to the affirmative.

"You're the best. That's why we hired you. We always want the best people working for us."

"And why did you feel like you needed the best? From the outside looking in, Liberty has everything under control."

"Absolutely," John agrees. "I believe we have. But we also have potential beyond the capabilities of our previous head of finance and with that in mind we decided to bring in someone who could handle what we hope the future will hold for us. It's all about growth mindset and you have the skill we will need as we grow."

I slump back in my chair and slowly exhale my sigh of relief, hoping John can't hear. He sounds perfectly genuine. I'm not being tested. I really have uncovered something that has been missed until now.

"So tell me what you have found," he urges.

"Okay." I sit forward and scroll through the spreadsheet open on my screen. "I was putting together a proposal for a new expense reporting system for you and Mr. McAllister to take a look at, when I started noticing that many expense claims which have been approved over the last financial year were not included on the employees' actual expense reports."

There is a long pause.

"Staff submit expense reports each month to their department and the department managers sign off on them and submit them to finance, right?"

"Correct."

"So, all requests would have a manager's signature before they come to finance?"

"Unless they exceed the department limit or are somehow special in circumstance, yes I believe so," John confirms.

"And those over-limits or special circumstances would still be verified with receipts and signed off by a finance manager. Correct?"

"Yes, absolutely."

"So any time there is 'special authorization', I should be seeing more supporting documentation, not less."

"And you're not?"

"No..." I drift off as I scroll and think about what I'm really seeing here. I'd had a bad feeling, but voicing my concerns aloud have cemented my worst fears. "I think someone is stealing from the company," I tell him cautiously, unsure of how this will go down.

"Who?"

"Questionable transactions appear in the expense reports of nearly half the staff on the payroll. But every single suspicious entry has the same characteristics. All are large amounts. All have bypassed department managers and been authorized directly by finance and have no receipts or other documentation on file. And they were all authorized by the same Work ID."

"Who is it, Charlotte?" John demands.

"It says ELISKIN. I don't know who that is."

John curses sharply under his breath. Honestly, I'm tempted to join him.

"I'm not even through the second quarter of last year, but this is big. We need to act quickly. Whoever this is needs to be suspended immediately while we investigate. We need to involve the police."

"Just hold on, Charlotte. Slow down."

"Why? It's critical that we collect evidence and press charges as soon as possible. I don't think you realize the kind of money we're talking about here and it's probably still happening. We have to end it now." As I'm speaking, I pull up this month's company-wide travel and expense report to see what is happening right now. I change the filter to search specifically for expenses authorized by ELISKIN, but before I hit enter, John stops me.

"It's not still happening, Charlotte. She no longer works for the company."

My fingers hover over the enter key. "For how long?"

"A few weeks. Technically, you replaced her."

"I see." I clear the search, knowing I won't find anything in this month and pull up last month instead. "I've got to tell you, you don't sound shocked, John."

I can hear his long release of breath. "Is it possible to be deeply shocked and not at all surprised at the same time?"

"I think it must be because that's exactly how you sound." I tap my pen on my desk thinking. "Look, we need to report this to Mr. McAllister. The sooner the better. He will want to press charges."

"I will call him as soon as I get off the line," John tells me.

"If an accusation is going to be made, I think it should come from me, don't you? It's not exactly the kind of meeting I want to be our first, but it needs to be."

"Charlotte, I appreciate what you're saying, but this matter needs to be handled...delicately."

Scowling at the phone on my desk, I prepare to fight my corner. "And why is that?"

"Miss King, the former employee in question, is a...personal friend of Mr. McAllister's."

*"So you mean he's fucking her?"* is right on the tip of my tongue, but I hold it in.

"Their families are friends," he tries to assert, but the damage has been done. It's obvious Mr. McAllister is, or at least was, tangled up with her in a less than professional manner. The dumbass. Doesn't he know, you don't shit where you eat?

"Well he should know that his 'friend' has been ripping him off as soon as possible then, don't you think?"

"I will call him and let him know what you've found. For now, if you could just gather all the information..."

"Sure," I cut him off, applying more sass than is professional, but seriously? "I think you should know though, this could be in the millions by the time I'm through."

"Christ," he hisses. "I'll call him now."

He ends the call, promising to come see me in the morning to brief me on whatever Mr. McAllister decides to do.

Just as I am going to dive back into my reports my cell chimes. I sigh, it's probably Louise wanting to go out after work. It is Friday night after all, but I don't think I can handle Cami after the day I've had. Picking up my phone and opening it however, I smile when I see it's a message from Michael. We've been texting with each other a little since our pseudo-date last week.

**Michael:** How's your Friday?

**Me:** It's been interesting...

**Michael:** Oh? Do tell...

**Me**: Let's just say you were right.

**Michael:** Three words I love to hear! About what specifically?

I glance at my screen and feel the weight of this problem press down on me. I need to leave it behind when I go home or it's going to dominate my whole weekend.

**Me:** Work stuff. Long story, I'll fill you in later.

**Michael:** Sounds ominous! Want to meet for drinks?

I think about it for a moment.

**Me:** Thanks, but maybe another night. I've had a rough day. I probably wouldn't be much company.

**Michael:** I don't believe that. You would be good company on your worst day. I could play dirty and tempt you with BBQ.

**Me:** Ugh! You are evil.

**Michael:** To the core. But those ribs though...

**Me:** You are going to make me gain ten pounds.

**Michael:** They have salad if you're going to be a wuss about it.

**Me:** PFT! You had me at ribs. What time?

**Michael:** Can we say 8? I have some things to sort out first.

**Me:** Sure, but you have been warned, I'm offloading on you hard.

**Michael:** I'll do some stretches.

I giggle to myself. I like him, he's funny and good company.

I shove my phone aside and dive into the data that's calling my name. Pulling the numbers into a new spreadsheet makes it easier for me to sort through all the information. It's shows clearly how many of the entries by this ELISKIN person are fraudulent. She uses most of the female staff as her scapegoats, but there are some men in there too.

Once I start going through the entries I begin cross-referencing them against her personal corporate card and find the confirmation we need there in black and white. Even though she was entering the expenses under other names, she was using her card. And no one was checking because the buck stopped with her. And I'm fairly certain she was fucking the boss.

"Ugh!" Was she even qualified to do the job? I bet she wasn't. And now I'm left clearing up the mess.

As I'm going through her statements, I happen to notice that her card is still active and there have been cash withdrawals since she left. A lot of cash withdrawals! I snort. Not for long, Missy. I mark her card as inactive immediately. This girl has an expensive shopping habit, designer brands, luxury goods and Lord knows what else with her cash withdrawals and she isn't doing it on Liberty's dime any longer. Let her take it up with her boyfriend.

After a couple more hours of cross-referencing, I notice the time. It's past six, I need to go home. I've had as much as I can take for one day and I need to go get ready to meet Michael. My stomach rumbles at the thought of dinner. Saving my separate file as ELISKIN, I shut everything down and swear to myself I won't log into it again until Monday morning.

# NINE

"Well, well." Connor grins. "Back again."

"I can't keep away now. I know how good your ribs are." I wink.

"I bet you say that to all the boys." He laughs, then nods his head toward the back of the restaurant. "He's in back, come on."

I follow him through and as I approach the booth Michael stands to greet me.

"Look who I found," Connor teases Michael. "Kept that quiet didn't you."

"I don't run my every move past you, you know." He rolls his eyes, before turning his attention to me kissing my cheek. "You look lovely."

"Thanks, so do you." I wince at the way I returned the compliment. Is it weird to call him lovely?

"Why thank you," Conner replies behind me before I can overanalyze it and I turn to find him preening and laughing accepting the compliment happily since he's the carbon copy of his brother.

Michael shakes his head and ushers me into his booth.

"What can I get you to drink, Charlotte? Another cider?" Connor takes out his pad and I notice for the first time that he has tattoos on both forearms. He must have been wearing longer sleeves last time because he is covered in them. Immediately, I think of Rhys. I don't know what it is about me noticing all these hot tattooed men all of a sudden. I typically go for a much more sophisticated look. Like Michael... "Charlotte?" He snaps his fingers in front of my eyes.

Good Lord, pull yourself together! "You know, I think I need something a little stronger." I scan the menu. "I'll have a Martini, dirty."

"Rough day, huh?" he asks, scribbling the order down.

"You could say that."

"Then this one is on me," he says.

"Oh no, you don't have to do that."

"I insist, a thank you for getting this guy out of the house." He points his pencil at Michael.

Michael groans and Connor takes his leave before Michael has anything to say.

"Sorry about him," he offers.

I wave him off. "He obviously cares about you."

"There's caring and then there's Connor," he scoffs, but he has affection in his eyes.

"I think it's sweet that you're close."

"How about you? Are you close with your family?"

"I'm an only child and my parents both passed."

"I'm so sorry."

"It's okay. It was a very long time ago." I shrug it off.

"Still..."

I nod.

Connor returns with our drinks, breaking the gloom, and sets them down. "Are we going big again, guys?"

"I don't know." Michael looks to me. "Think you can handle it again?"

"It was a lot of food. But the leftovers were good."

"Right on it." Connor doesn't give us a chance to hesitate a second longer and walks away. I can't help that my eyes follow him as he leaves the table. The rear is just as perfect as the front. I wonder if he has any ink back there...

Michael clears his throat and laughs awkwardly. "He's an asshole you know."

I smirk, busted. "He seems okay to me."

"You're something you know that?"

"What do you mean?"

"Never mind me, you just carry on checking out my brother."

"In my defense, he's your identical twin brother."

"I promise you, we are very different."

"I can see that." I eye his forearms and struggling to imagine any ink under those sleeves.

He scowls. "I could have tattoos you know."

"Do you though?"

"That's beside the point."

I lift my drink. "You're funny when you get huffy."

"Women are just suckers for muscles and tattoos aren't you?"

I slowly shake my head, showing my amusement. "You are both extremely handsome in very different ways. Is that better? Although, I'm quite sure you both hear it enough, especially since when you stand beside each other the effect is amplified tenfold."

Michael leans forward on his elbows and picks up his beer. "It never gets old though."

It feels like we are having a moment, but there is less certainty in his eyes than before.

"So tell me about your week," he says, changing the subject. "I was right was I?"

He genuinely seems to care how my week went, so I start

dumping it all on him. He listens to how frustrated I am that there isn't any sense of urgency, or even alarm and how I suspect she was fucking the boss.

"You have to think, it's ultimately his money she stole. Maybe he knew the entire time and just didn't care. Either way it isn't your company, or your problem. You are just doing a job."

"I didn't think about it that way, you're right. I'm not accountable and this is out of my control. Thank you."

"What are friends for?" He hesitates and I nod in understanding. There it is...the entrance to the friend zone. I have to admit, I felt like we were headed there myself, but I don't know, I'm just trying this dating thing out and I guess it would have been nice to feel a little more desired before we got there.

Michael shifts uncomfortably in his seat and I catch the movement of his left thumb as it rubs over his finger. And there, sitting proudly on his ring finger, is a gold band I hadn't noticed before. His hand stills and I look up at him.

There is no way Cami would have tried to set me up with a married man...is there?

Michael lets out a sigh and then puts his left hand under the table out of sight. "I'm sorry, if I can't even take my wedding band off, perhaps I shouldn't be here."

"Recently divorced?" I ask hopefully. It's the lesser of the evils I could be faced with I guess.

"No—" He almost adds something else, then changes his mind and presses his lips together.

"Should we just call it a night?" I ask reluctantly.

He has the saddest look on his face and I'm not sure what I can do about it. But before I can say anything else, he straightens and takes a deep breath. "No. I want to have dinner with you," he says with a fierce determination in his voice.

"I just need to know one thing. Is she still in the picture?" Friend zone or not, I will not sit and flirt with another woman's husband if she is still in the picture. Not after how my own marriage ended.

"She passed away five years ago."

My heart drops. Oh shit. "I'm so sorry." I reach my hand across the table and give his a squeeze.

He brings his other hand up to join them and for a moment we both just stare at the poignant reminder he wears every day.

"My brother told me to take it off a long time ago, I just... can't."

"I understand."

He squeezes my hand, grateful for my understanding. "I'm not ready for a relationship. I'm still grieving. But having met you, I know I'm sure as hell ready for a friend. I wouldn't have agreed to a blind date if I'd known that's what it was, but I'm really glad it happened because I want to get to know you. I think we could be great friends." He lowers his eyes for a moment. "God that sounded like the worst brush off of all time, I'm so sorry. I—"

"Michael." I stop him. He looks up at me and I can't help but giggle. "Sorry, I'm not laughing at you. It's just, fucking Cami. She's a disaster!"

Michael chuckles too. "Right? I'm sorry you got caught up in my mess."

"Hey no, no more apologies. The truth is, I'm probably not ready for a relationship either. I don't know. But I would love to be your friend. You are my first new friend in London. I'm happy we met and I want to get to know you too."

"Good." He lets go of my hands and takes a long drink. "So what's your story?"

I guess fair's, fair. "I married my high school sweetheart, he cheated on me and we divorced. I just haven't gotten back in the saddle yet."

"How long has it been?"

"About five years."

"Wow. You must have really loved him."

"Why do you say that?"

"Five years and you haven't got back in the saddle, I just figured you were still hung up."

I sigh. "It wasn't that at all. It was over years before he cheated, I was just too into my work to do anything about it. I let it happen, my company was my first priority."

"Marriage is hard work, you either grow with the person or you grow apart."

"That's the truth right there." I sigh.

"We are a pair aren't we?"

"It feels like we've been friends for longer than a week," I agree.

"Cheers to that," he says, lifting his drink. We clink glasses and both take a sip just as a waitress comes and sets down our platter. "And for the record, I think you are ready."

"You do? What gives you that impression?"

"I don't know really, just a feeling. I think if the right guy came along and swept you off your feet, you'd be ready to love again."

"Hmm."

"You don't agree?"

"I don't know. I always just assumed that because I had no desire to go about looking for love, that meant I wasn't ready. Don't you think if I was I'd be out there hunting me a man?"

Michael lets out a hearty laugh which lights up his eyes and it makes me smile to know despite all he has been through I am able to bring that smile to his face. "Not really, I'm a firm believer that if something is meant to be, then it will happen whether you are looking for it or not. That's how I met my wife. She literally ran into me." His eyes brighten when he mentions her, then his expression changes. "Sorry."

"Don't be afraid to talk about her to me, she's part of you, Michael. Own her, Christ flaunt her." I lift my martini and tap it once again to his beer. "Cheers, to..." I pause, realizing I don't even know her name.

"Katherine, her name was Katherine." His face softens and he smiles fondly.

"Cheers to Katherine."

"Thank you, Charlotte." He sets his drink down. "It feels good to say her name. Connor loved her but he wants me to move on and be happy. It's gotten so that I watch how often I mention her because he takes it to mean I'm not living my life."

"That's crazy. She was your wife. You're going to think about her and talk about her forever. That's how it should be."

"I know. He knows that too. He just worries about me, you know?"

"I know. So that's why he was so giddy you were on a second date?"

"Yeah. I'm afraid of how he will take it when I kill his dream now."

"He doesn't have to know you friend zoned me." A wicked smirk spreads across my face as Michael stutters his defense.

"I didn't— You— It's just—"

I can't help but laugh. "I'm teasing. We friend zoned each other."

"You're wicked. But I like your style, he won't know we aren't dating romantically. He'll just be over the moon I'm seeing someone. This is brilliant, you're an evil genius."

"I'm happy to be of service. We should set up our next 'date' and make sure he knows about it before we leave."

"Yeah." Michael looks slightly resigned. "I shouldn't need to prove to him that I'm moving on. He cares and all, but he's been pushing way too hard. You know he threatened to cut my ring off while I'm sleeping?"

I gasp. "No! You'll take it off if and when you're ready. Don't let anyone tell you when that should be."

"He's probably right. It just feels wrong."

"The thing is Michael, you took vows. Ones that you're obviously having a hard time setting aside even if she's gone. No one has the right to tell you when you should be ready to move on or if you should ever even want to move on. It's your life."

"Thanks, Charlotte." He sips his beer. "It's getting easier since we left Chicago."

"Is that why you moved here?"

"Yeah, it wasn't healthy for me, I couldn't move on when everywhere in the city reminded me of us. We met in school there, she was from here actually on a one-year transfer as part of her degree. But she wound up staying. That city was ours. We met there, dated there, married there. I realized I was never going to be able to stop grieving when I was suffocating on thoughts of her just driving down the street."

"Well, it sounds like you did the right thing for yourself by moving away."

Michael looks up at me, seeming guilty somehow. "I didn't just do it for me," he says softly.

I frown, not understanding who else he could have done it for.

Michael reaches into his pocket and pulls out his wallet, opening it quickly and pulling out a piece of paper. He looks at it for a long moment before handing it to me. "She has her mama's eyes," he says as I take in the face of a darling little girl. Dark curls like her dad and a cheeky smile.

I touch my fingers to my lips, understanding the full extent of this man's grief at last. He didn't just lose his wife, he's a dad and he's doing it all alone.

"She's beautiful," I whisper.

"Thank you." He smiles, taking back the photo and gazing at

it once more before tucking it safely back into his wallet. I watch him, not knowing which of my questions is even appropriate to ask, when he begins speaking.

"Her name is Katie," he says. "After she was born Katherine told me she wanted to come back here. Raise her here. We hadn't really talked about moving here before that, she was happy in Chicago. We both had good jobs, we lived in a good neighborhood. But when they put her in Katherine's arms she changed. She was so full of love for this little thing and it came pouring out. How she wanted to raise her where she grew up, send her to the school she went to, push her on the swing in the playground she knew as a child..."

He drifts off and I can't help the direction my thoughts are going, so I ask. "And you didn't want that?"

His eyes snap to mine. "No, I thought it sounded fantastic. As I said, we hadn't talked about it before that moment, but with this tiny thing between us that we suddenly loved more than we knew possible, we laid squished into her hospital bed, and we talked and talked. I felt it too, Chicago is an amazing city until you have this most precious thing to take care of and suddenly all I kept thinking was, 'murder capital of the United States', on repeat like that ticker on the bottom of the screen on the news channel. It was crazy the shift in our thinking, but we both agreed, England would be the best place for us to be. Our hope was to move before she started school. We made so many plans that day..."

"But she—" I don't even know what I was going to ask, but I stop myself.

"But she didn't get to carry any of them out. She never got to see Katie's smile or hear her laugh." He pauses and swallows hard. "She never even got to take her home."

I inhale deeply and wait. Knowing the worst part is still to come, but I have to let him tell me. We are friends after all.

"She died six hours and forty-three minutes after Katie was born. Blood clot."

"God, I am so sorry." I breathe, letting out all the air I was holding.

"Those were the best six hours and forty-three minutes of our lives. She was so happy. So full of life and plans for the future. Being a mom lit her up like I had never seen and I would have given her anything she asked for in those hours. She wanted to move here, and raise Katie right where she was raised and I was all in. I would have moved to the moon for her."

"So you kept your promise?" I ask softly, trying not to choke on the emotion constricting my throat and keep the threatening tears at bay.

Michael nods. "There was nothing left for me in Chicago and I needed to get away. So I kept my promise."

"And Connor came to."

Michael scratches at his beard and huffs out a half laugh. "Connor had his own reasons for wanting to get out of Chicago, but he'll tell you he was only looking out for me. It made our parents happier too. They really didn't want me to go. But they respected my decision, and Connor gets to be the good son for once by acting as their eyes and ears."

"Wow," I say.

"Yeah, sorry. I should have warned you, I can be really terrible company."

"No, not at all. I'm glad you told me. I was just thinking how brave that was. I thought I was ballsy moving here, but moving to a new country with a toddler and doing it all alone?"

"I'm not really alone. I have Connor. He's more use than he looks, but don't tell him I said that. And we live close to Katherine's parents. They really help out. I couldn't do it without them to be honest. It's been hard, but we have a great relationship and they love Katie so much."

"I bet they do. Is that who she's with now?"

"Yes, they help out after school and usually have her at least one night a week. They want me to have a life too, although they're slightly more subtle about it than Connor."

"So they know you are on a 'date'?" I use air quotes to define what this now is.

Michael presses his lips together, looking guilty again, but this time with more humor. "I told them I was meeting a friend after work."

"I see how it is, you had me friend zoned before you even got here."

"Hey now." He smiles for the first time since opening up about his life. "We friend zoned each other. You agreed."

We continue to laugh after that. The conversation turns to the superficial things we miss about home and what we love about London. We make a small dent in the mountain of food between us and when we look beat, the waitress comes around.

"Can I get you guys anything?" she asks, eyeing our leftovers skeptically.

I hold my stomach and groan. "I can't eat another thing."

"Just two to-go boxes please, and we'll take the check whenever you're ready." Michael's smile is all charm. I notice the waitress flush slightly as she leaves to get the check.

When she returns with our boxes and the check I remind Michael firmly that we agreed I would pay for this one and while I pay, he asks the waitress how her shift has been. I hand back the card machine and he tells her he will see her again soon. She grins and looks away, a more definite pinkish blush staining her cheeks. The man is clearly not aware of the effect he has on women.

I sit back grinning and he turns his gaze back to me, his eyes narrowing slightly before he speaks, "What?"

"You have no idea what you're doing do you?"

His brows furrow. "Doing? What am I doing?" He stands to leave while still looking confused.

I simply smile and stand, collecting my jacket, then turn to walk out of the restaurant.

Michael follows close behind me. "Are you going to fill me in?"

The waitress in question is too close by and I don't want to embarrass the poor girl, so I keep walking toward the door.

Michael makes it around me and holds the door open for me to go through. Then he looks expectantly. "So?"

"The waitress thought you were flirting with her, that's why she started turning pink."

"No! I was not. I wouldn't do that on a date even if it is with just a friend."

I laugh at his flustered indignation. "That's what makes it even funnier. You have no clue you're doing it."

"I guess I should watch that. I thought I was just being polite."

We start to walk down the Soho side street heading for the busier areas to make our way home.

"You don't have to watch anything," I tell him. "I think it's cute and they love it."

"I don't want to give off the wrong signals though."

I pause and watch him for a moment. "You know, you were right about something. If something is meant to be, then it will happen whether you are looking for it or not. Don't change who you are, who says they are the wrong signals? Maybe one day you'll give just the right signal to just the right person and everything will change."

Michael's gaze intensifies as he steps toward me. He takes me by the elbow and pulls me in close to him. I laugh and begin to tell him I didn't mean with me, when I suddenly find myself against his chest and looking up into his serious blue eyes.

"Charlotte..." he whispers and sets his lips on mine.

Our lips touch softly and for a moment I sink into the warmth of him, until he pulls away without deepening the connection.

The second he pulls back I frown, touching my lips. I expect to feel something there. Some spark or zing marking the place he had been, but, nothing.

"Don't be mad," he says apologetically. "I had to see." He reaches out to my arm, squeezing softly. "Did you feel anything?"

"I—" I don't want to hurt him.

"I felt nothing," he admits. "I'm sorry. Do you think I'm broken?"

"No, I think we are just truly meant to be friends."

We both stare into each other's eyes for a moment and then burst out laughing.

"Well at least we got that out of the way. There will be no 'what if' thinking." Michael runs his hands through his hair.

"If it makes you feel better, I was secretly wondering if there would have been any spark between us too."

"Well I guess now we know." He offers me his crooked elbow. "Shall we?"

I slip my arm through his and we start walking again, only to bump straight into a woman in a hurry, not watching where she's walking.

"Ugh," she huffs irritably as if we were somehow to blame for her walking and texting. She looks up and I inwardly groan.

"Well if it isn't Little Miss America. It's no surprise to see you here I suppose," she sneers, looking beyond us at the BBQ joint with distain. I wonder if she's ever eaten anything off-the-bone in her life. That is if she even ingests anything but coke and gin.

"Hello Lisa," I grit out. "Fancy seeing you here. You seem in a hurry, doesn't your dealer like to be kept waiting?" Ugh I hate that she makes me sound so petty but this bitch really gets my back up.

She answers my jibe with a scathing look and a determination not to take the bait that I can see pains her. Instead, she gives Michael a once-over and a cold smile crosses her face. "If you ever want to have dinner with a refined woman..."

Michael smiles back, a look I can tell even having only known him a short time, says he's up to no good. "Well now, darlin'," he drawls exaggeratedly. "I just had a mighty fine dinner with this swell little lady right here." My eyes bug out as I try to hold the laugher in. Michael pats his stomach. "Now I'm fixin' to head on home. But head on inside, darlin', you look as if you could use a good meal."

"Ugh!" She flips her hair and pushes past us, muttering, "Americans." Leaving us both unable to keep our laughter under control.

"You are so bad," I scold, slapping his chest playfully.

He pulls me in under his arm fondly and starts walking again. "Why I don't know what you mean, darlin'," he quips.

Beside us, on the otherwise quiet street, a car that was parked fires up and squeals away.

"Everyone's in such a hurry tonight," Michael says as we turn the corner.

# TEN

**Michael:** Did you leave yet?

**Me:** Yeah, I'm at the bar. They won't seat me until my whole party is here. *eyeroll*

**Michael:** Oh God, now I feel even worse.

**Me:** What's up?

I sit up on my stool worrying for him.

**Michael:** Nothing major. Katie is running a fever and I'm heading home. My in-laws were happy to keep her but she wants me.

I clutch my chest, staring at the phone. God he's so sweet. I can't even get annoyed at being stood up.

**Me:** I completely understand. You go home and make your girl feel better. We can have dinner next week.

**Michael:** I still feel like an asshole. I bet you're wishing we'd made plans to have BBQ again, then at least Connor would look after you.

**Me:** Honestly, I don't mind. I'll just head home and take my bra off.

**Michael:** LOL Okay. I'll make it up to you. I promise.

**Me:** Hope Katie feels better.

**Michael:** Enjoy your bra free night.

I stare down at my phone, trying to decide what to do now. I'll just pay for my drink and head out. I can pick up some food on my way home. Maybe Louise would like me to bring her something. I wince, she'll probably have Cami with her, and suddenly the idea of a night in seems less appealing. I decide to text her and find out which direction my evening is about to take a turn for.

**Me:** You home?

**Louise:** No, I'm at Cami's for the night.

**Me:** Oh, okay.

I try not to do any kind of visible celebrations. A quiet night by myself it is.

**Louise:** You know, I can tell even by text when you really mean 'thank fuck for that'!

I snort a little. I know she can read me but the way she just says it like that makes me laugh out loud.

**Me:** I'm heading home, I just wanted to know if you wanted me to bring you dinner.

**Louise:** Thought you were having dinner out?

**Me:** I was. Plans changed.

I haven't told her that my dinner was with Michael, nor do I feel like explaining that I'm in the restaurant and got stood up. It just makes too much out of the situation.

**Louise:** Sorry, want me to come home?

**Me:** No! Don't be silly.

God, if she comes home she will have Cami with her, and no bra is only appealing without a side of Cami.

**Louise:** LMAO! I get the hint. Have a good (and peaceful) evening.

"Oh I will" I say out loud, already anticipating the relief.

"Are you talking to yourself, kitten?"

I feel the goose pimples pop up under my sweater. Something about that deep voice and accent drives me wild. I'm just not sure if it's with annoyance or desire. Setting my phone down I look up. "Rhys. Nice to see you."

"Pleasant surprise to see you too. Are you having a quiet supper alone?"

"I was stood up," I admit, then curse my honesty.

He barks a laugh. "No shit? You should join me." He indicates an empty table a few feet away against the wall and I wonder how long he has been there. I didn't notice him when I arrived.

I raise a brow. "*You* are dining alone, Rhys?"

"Sheath those claws, kitten, I dine alone from time to time. Tonight I had a meeting which happened to be resolved over the first drink, so now I find myself lacking a dinner companion. Coincidence, no?" He raises a brow back at me.

"What would Lisa think of you having dinner with another woman?"

"That's what I like about you, kitten, you say what you mean."

"You don't know me that well." Taking another sip of my martini, I'm torn between setting the drink aside or gulping it down.

"I know enough to want to get to know you better." He holds out his hand, urging me to join him.

I stare at him, extremely torn. I want to be unavailable, leave and protect myself from whatever feeling keeps sparking up whenever I run into him. Then on the other hand, I'm here, I need to eat and he's alone. No Lisa. What harm would dinner do?

"Come on, kitten," he whispers. "You know you want to."

I roll my eyes, but stand up against my better judgement. I collect my drink and purse and reluctantly take his still outstretched hand. The moment his fingers touch mine, something ignites inside me I thought was long dead. Oh man I say to myself.

He keeps hold of my hand until I'm lowered into my chair and then leans down to press a kiss to my knuckles before letting it go. I whip it back and rub at the spot that is prickling from the contact as he rounds the table chuckling to himself.

"You didn't answer my question," I say, trying to cover my reaction, but the breathy rasp of my voice marks my attempt to cover as a fail.

He looks at me with those intense blue eyes, and I feel like they are searing my soul or at least trying to reach into the depths of my mind.

"Lisa would not like us having dinner together was the question? No."

I put down my drink with finality. "Right. So I should probably go."

The corner of his mouth tilts up. "I'd like you to stay," he says, reaching for my hand across the table before I can stand. "Lisa doesn't have a say in who I have dinner with. She doesn't have a say in anything." His tone has a hint of regret. Perhaps he didn't want to break up.

"I'm sorry."

"Are you really, kitten?"

He's calling my bluff and I laugh. "No, no I'm not. She's not a very nice person."

"There's the Charlotte I met at the airport," he laughs. "Lisa is nice sometimes, when she wants something."

"Very commendable, Rhys."

"What is?"

"Even though she wasn't very nice you aren't bad-mouthing

her when I gave you the perfect opportunity to." It puts him a notch higher in my book.

"Fair enough. She's in the past and that's where I would like her to stay."

I raise my glass. "Cheers to that."

"I'm famished," he says, reaching for the menu and giving it a cursory glance. Something tells me this is somewhere he knows.

"Is the food good?"

"Very good. The perfect place for a romantic evening." He wears an amused grin. "I guess your date disagreed."

I ignore the dig because I'd rather he thought I was dating, even if I was stood up, than meeting a friend because I have no love life. Instead I tell him a half-truth. "He had an emergency, he called in plenty of time to let me know, but... I'm an early bird. I was already here." I lift my drink and watch him over the rim as I take a sip. "Then, there you were."

"That seems to be happening to us a lot."

Indeed.

My phone buzzes on the table, accompanied by the faint ping of a text since I have the volume down way low. I ignore it. It won't be Michael and Louise is wrapped up in Cami, so I'm not interested in who it could be.

Rhys looks at it, but follows my lead in ignoring it. Although, I can see it gnawing at him. I'm sure he thinks it's my 'date'. Then without warning it starts ringing. This I can't ignore. Even though the volume is way down low, there's no mistaking the ringtone. I don't even bother looking at the screen as I pick it up, the ringtone is just for her. I rarely get to hear it since we mostly text, so I had almost forgotten. It's Beyoncé's "Flawless." I decline the call and set my phone back down.

"Don't you need to get that?" He frowns.

"Nope, it's my best friend. I'm staying with her so I can talk to her later."

"Won't she worry?"

"I'm a big girl. She's doing her thing. I told her my plans changed and I was heading home, but she's out for the evening so she won't even notice."

"Well that wasn't a smart idea."

"Why?"

"Well first of all, if you told her you were going home, you should let her know your plans changed again or she could be worried."

I fold my arms across my chest and look at him getting worked up. "And second?"

"Second, you shouldn't be out on a date at all without someone knowing exactly where you are. It's careless."

I stifle a laugh.

"It's not funny. Anything could happen."

"Like getting picked up by a man who seems to be everywhere, like a kind of stalker you mean?"

A slow, knowing smile creeps onto his face. "Touché, kitten." He reaches for his drink, something amber on the rocks. "Still you should let her know you aren't going home yet. I would feel better if you did."

"Remove you as a suspect you mean?"

"Something like that."

I lift my phone and read the notifications on screen.

**Louise:** I'm heading home after all. Long story! Just wanted to give you a heads-up in case you were wandering around in your birthday suit.

**Missed call from Louise.**

**Louise:** I tried calling you, are you lost on the tube or lying in a gutter?

"Jesus," I hiss under my breath, feeling the pressure. I haven't had to answer to anyone in years, now I'm getting nagged from all sides.

**Me:** Met another friend.

"What are you telling her?"

It's like he knows I have no plans to tell her who I'm with. "I told her I met another friend."

My phone buzzes, I groan to myself.

"She's a good friend, worrying about you."

"Nosy is more like it."

My phone goes off again. "Christ."

"Why don't you read her message?" He glances down at my phone which is face down on the table and in the process of buzzing again.

I turn it over and glance at the screen. "She wants to know who I am with."

"Why don't you just tell her?"

"It's none of her business. Besides, she wouldn't believe it if I told her." God I can just see her freaking out and then Cami will be insufferable.

"No? Why's that?" he asks, frowning.

My phone goes off again, saving me from answering him. He chuckles as he gets up and takes the chair next to me.

"Do you mind?" he asks, pointing to my phone.

"By all means." I push the phone over to him, assuming he wants to read the newest messages. He moves his chair close to mine so we are side by side and my heart starts racing. Looking down at my phone, he turns the camera on and reverses it for a selfie.

"What are you doing?" I jerk back in surprise.

"Making her believe you," he replies innocently. "Smile," he says as he lifts the phone up framing us in the picture. I muster up the best smile I can, one that reaches my eyes so Louise doesn't come running to the restaurant to save me. A second before he presses the button though, he turns his head and kisses my cheek.

"Shit, don't send that," I gasp, reaching for my phone.

He chuckles. "Come on, look how cute we look. It's a good photo."

I'll admit it's a good photo and the look on my face. Christ I'm already dreading the Spanish inquisition when I get home. "She'll freak out, we look like a couple."

"I know." His grin gets bigger and he hits send.

I groan. "Do you have any idea what you just did?"

"I sure do. You'll be talking about me for days. I'll enjoy knowing my name is rolling off your tongue." He says the last so softly near my ear that I shiver as the whisper of breath raises the hairs on my arms.

I shake my head and feel my face heat.

"Are you ready to order?" a voice breaks the haze Rhys put me into.

"I am, are you, kitten?" He remains in the chair close to mine and I find myself not minding, if anything, wanting to get even closer.

He is a complication I do not need in my life.

"I'll have the fish and chips," he tells the waiter.

My phone buzzes on the table. Rhys smiles even bigger if that's possible.

"I'll have the same please," I add, knowing I'm too distracted to read a menu properly anyway. The waiter vanishes as fast as he came.

"Kitten, if I had problems with seizures, your phone would trigger one." He laughs again.

"Ughh! Stop laughing, she's probably freaking out right now." I say as yet another hum sounds from my phone.

"Read her texts and see."

Curiosity is getting the better of me and I relent. I want to see what she has to say, since she keeps firing messages.

**Louise:** OMG

**Louise:** Are you joking?

**Louise:** Should I be worried?

**Louise:** Okay I am worried.

**Louise:** ANSWER ME!!!

"See what you started? What the hell am I going to say to her?"

"You are a grown woman. How about you tell her you'll talk to her after dinner?"

"Good idea, maybe then she will leave me alone."

**Me:** We'll talk when I get home. x

I place my phone on do not disturb so I don't get hammered with twenty more questions. I can deal with them later. For now I am just going to enjoy my meal.

"So, what do you do for work?" I try and get the conversation moving away from my nosy friend.

"I own a few businesses and I like to play in the stock market. What about you?" He takes hold of my hand that was on the table and plays with it like it belongs to him, he strokes down my palm making me shiver. I pull it back in order to maintain some control.

"I am a CFO, figures and expenses are my thing."

The waiter comes and drops off the food at our table. The service was fast, not that I'm going to complain, the sooner we're done eating, the quicker I can make a beeline out of here.

Our meal passes with some easier than expected conversation. Rhys didn't move back across from me, but stayed seated close where I swear he's brushed his leg up against mine on purpose around a hundred times.

Before I know it, the waiter sets the check down. I guess time flies in good company. Without missing a beat, Rhys takes out his card.

"I'll be right back with the machine," the waiter says, disappearing.

"I can pay for my own, we should go halfsies."

"No way, kitten, I've had a lovely time with you. My treat. I'd like to go out with you again in fact."

I pause and think about it for a second, but my mouth is working before my brain can analyze it. "I'd like that," I tell him almost involuntarily.

"Good. Oh and will you text me that picture?" He smirks as he pays, having distracted me from the bill situation, and smoothly he writes down his number on the receipt for me.

I shove it in my purse. "Sure," I reply with a shrug.

He helps me out of my seat and we walk toward the door of the restaurant. I pause in the street to say goodbye.

"Which way is home?" he asks.

"The tube stop is only a block away." I point toward the underground sign glowing in the darkness.

"I'll make sure you get home." He slides his hand into mine and fireworks ignite where we touch.

"It's not that late. I'll be fine." I try to extract my hand to stop the feeling but he only holds me tighter.

"I insist." Giving my hand a playful tug, he sets off toward the station.

"I'm a big girl, Rhys, nothing is going to happen to me."

One second we're walking and the next I'm pushed against a building in an alleyway I hadn't even seen, Rhys pressing his body into mine.

I gasp and look up into his determined eyes glinting in the darkness.

"Anything can happen in a split second."

My eyes focus on his lips, perfect and full. I lick mine as I think about how they would feel there. "Point taken," I murmur.

His stare never leaves me and his breaths are as heavy as my own. His body feels hard everywhere he touches me, while his hands cage me in against the wall. I close my eyes, soaking in the feeling of him surrounding me completely.

"Open your eyes, kitten."

His low command makes me shiver as I slowly obey. I try to break his fierce gaze, looking down. He moves a hand to my chin and guides my head back up. I swallow hard, my senses in overload as his fingers then trail down my throat, possessively. I feel a deep longing when my eyes settle on his tempting mouth, I run my teeth over my own bottom lip in response. He doesn't miss it. He watches the action hungrily, then leans in closer. I tense when his nose brushes over my ear.

"What do you want?" he whispers.

I swear I can already feel the heat of his lips on me even though he's still a breath away. I can't speak, I don't know what I want. Well, I do but I can't voice it. I shouldn't succumb to the need. Because I suspect that giving in to Rhys would be giving myself over to him completely, and that feels like something that could not be undone.

"Tell me," he demands, brushing his thumb across my lower lip.

"I can't." My words are barely audible, but he hears them.

"Yes you can, kitten. Say the word." He holds himself perfectly still, but he is all I feel, all I want in this moment, despite myself.

"You," I gasp, unable to stop myself. The word is carried forth on the surge of need rushing through my body. Feelings I haven't had in— oh who am I kidding— it's never felt this way.

"Me. What?" Rhys prompts.

"You," I repeat, still lost in the unfamiliar feelings.

"You'll have to be more specific, kitten." His lips curl up in a smirk and still linger too far from where I want them, but I don't want to— I can't beg.

"God Rhys, just take it," I snap.

He frames my face with both hands, not moving an inch away from me. "No," he says firmly. He reaches up and slips the clip out of my hair, letting it fall all around my shoulders and studying the result with interest. He strokes a few stray strands out of my face, almost reverently. He seems satisfied with his effort when he looks back into my eyes. "I'm not taking anything. You'll give it to me, Charlotte. Now, tell me what you want."

"I want you, Rhys," I cry, no longer caring who hears.

In a flash his lips take mine. I can't think, I can only feel him hard on me, devouring me. He deepens the kiss, his tongue as commanding as the man himself. I open to him willingly, bending to his will. I've never been kissed like this before.

Suddenly he breaks the kiss off and presses his forehead to mine, both of us breathing heavy. "Fuck, kitten, if I don't stop I'm going to take you right here."

I'm ripped from the bliss of surrender, aware of my surroundings again as the sounds of the busy street can once again be heard. Christ, what am I doing?

"Come home with me," Rhys asks tightly, sounding almost in his own battle with himself.

My heart races, the possibilities flash through my mind. But I have to be strong. "I can't."

Rhys looks at the ground for a beat, before looking back into my eyes. He searches for something there for a long moment, then nods his head, regretfully. "Okay, kitten," he says, stepping away. "Let's get you home."

# ELEVEN

Restless, that's how I slept.

I was damn lucky that Louise wasn't up when I left for work this morning. She is going to be all over this like a rash, and to make things worse, I'm not going to be able to hide my 'oh yeah, stuff definitely happened' face. She's going to know just from looking at me. I was better off in New York. At least I could hide my shit from her there. As if she knows I'm thinking her name, my phone chimes.

**Louise:** We need to catch up.

**Me:** Yeah yeah yeah...

With her message window open, I see the picture of Rhys and me from last night and my body instantly reacts to the sight of him. In the photo he's being silly, kissing my cheek, but I'm reminded of the feel of his hot breath on my skin and his lips caressing mine. I have to draw in a deep breath to cool myself off.

It's a great photo and I promised to send it to him. I could just forget all about it, but it seems I'm a glutton for punishment, because I'm reaching for my purse and pulling out his number before I can stop myself.

I hit send with a mixture of revulsion and excitement. Well then that's perfect isn't it, now he has my number.

A knock on my office door pulls me out of head. John is leaning on the doorframe and grateful for the interruption, I greet him eagerly. "John!"

"Hey, Charlotte." He smiles, stepping in.

"I hope you have news for me about what we are going to do about the missing funds."

I see him deflate slightly, his shoulders slump as he takes the chair across from me. "Mr. McAllister wants us to note the missing funds, settle the books and he will take it from there."

"What does that mean? He's going to press charges, right?" I fold my hands setting them on the desk.

"To be honest, Charlotte, I don't think he's going to do anything."

"What? That's a crock of shit," I snap, regretting my outburst immediately. "I apologize."

"No, I agree with you," John admits. "But it's Mr. McAllister's call and all we can do right now is the job he's asking us to do."

I suppress the desire to scoff. I must remain professional and he's right. "Well, that brings me to my next order of business," I tell him.

"I'm all ears." John sits back and crosses his legs.

I like the fact that he listens and has been taking my ideas. It's gratifying to know I'm valued despite the stuff with my predecessor.

"I want to completely overhaul the expense system effective immediately. I think we need to start over. There are too many opportunities to exploit it in its current state. Obviously the honor system has worked well until now, but the company is growing and the family it prides itself in being right now, won't always be as close knit. I think it's a good time to look at other systems and find one that gives us the security we need for the future."

John nods in thought for a few beats. Then he smiles. "You have my blessing," he says simply.

"Your blessing?" I frown. "Thanks. But I was hoping more for the green light from the top."

"Charlotte, the department is yours to run the way you see fit. Mr. McAllister trusts you. The lights are green all the way. Do what you think is best for Liberty."

I feel my brows creep up. I usually don't like to show surprise in the workplace because it feels like weakness, but really. "I'll tell you, I can't wait to meet him and find out what exactly I've done to earn this trust."

John shifts uncomfortably at my mention of meeting the evasive boss. "Indeed." Is all he can reply. "Now," he says in a much lighter tone, changing the subject completely. "How are you settling in to London life?"

"I love the city."

"Excellent. And your living arrangements?"

"Well, let's just say I love my best friend like a sister, but her romantic tastes leave a lot to be desired."

"Ah." John smiles knowingly. "Time to find your own place maybe?"

Sitting back in my chair, I sigh. "Perhaps."

"Well don't forget the offer I made."

I'd wanted to spend some time with Louise before I put down my own roots, but I don't blame her for the disruption to that plan. I did spring it on her that I was coming and she hadn't known that she would be diving fully into a new relationship at precisely that moment. Of course she wants to spend her time with Cami, who...isn't entirely bad. She's just a little full on for my liking and has boundary issues like you wouldn't believe. And if I get my own place, I'll see Louise plenty. I look up at John, who is patiently waiting for my thoughts to run their course. "How long of a waiting list is there to get into the building?" I finally ask.

"There is no wait for you. We had a newly vacated unit available when you interviewed and it has since been refurbished. I requested for it to be kept available for a few weeks until you were ready to consider it. I had a feeling that before long, you'd be in the market for your own place. I think it will be perfect for you."

"Seriously?" I think back to last night, when I had to sneak in after dinner with Rhys and then this morning when I left super early to avoid the questions. I think it's time I at least considered it. Not that I plan to make a habit of needing to sneak home after nights out of course. But if, I did ever, you know, have to do a walk of shame, at least there would be no one there to witness it. "Could I set up a viewing?"

"No need. I can show you. Would you like to go up now?"

I check my watch and note that it's only a little before noon, but if John is happy to take an early lunch to show me, I'm in. "Sure."

I grab my phone and my work badge, clipping it to my skirt. "Lead the way."

We walk through the office and out to the lobby. John pushes the button to go up. I'm excited. The building is nice and it would be convenient to live so close to work. The more I consider it, the more appealing it seems. I have to wait to see what the apartment is like before I set my heart on the whole idea.

"How did you like living here?" I ask, trying to rein myself in a little.

"We were very happy here. It suited us well. The building is secure. The landlord is reasonable." He smirks. "We only moved because our situation changed." He uses a special key to access the upper floors. "I honestly think you'll like it here."

"Do people from work drop by all the time?" I ask, voicing one of my concerns.

John chuckles as he shakes his head. "You don't have to worry about that. The office won't trouble you when you are off the clock. It's an unspoken rule. The tenants aren't all company employees, so your neighbors are just that, your neighbors. You can integrate with them as much as you please." He glances at me and chuckles again. "Or as little as you please. Seriously, Charlotte. It's no different than living in any other apartment building. You'll forget that it's in the same building as your office as soon as you pass the tenth floor."

As we travel through the floors, I make a mental note that I could take the stairs if I move in. I could use the workout, especially if I'm not going to be walking in from the tube station. We get off the elevator at the second to last floor and walk down a short hall. "It doesn't look like there are many units to a floor," I muse, following John.

"There aren't, only four on this floor."

"Are they all the same size?"

"No, the two end units are the biggest, aside from the penthouse." He stops in front of the door at the end and unlocks the door, pushing it open and standing aside for me to enter. "It's three bedrooms, fully furnished," he informs me as I pass.

The first thing I notice is how white and clean everything is. The ceilings are high and light floods the space, since glass makes up most of the external walls. A huge white sectional sofa filled with colorful throw pillows marks out the living area of the open space. Dark hardwood flooring runs throughout. I follow the room around to a big kitchen table with seating for eight, which separates the living area from a stunning kitchen with white marble countertops and white cabinets, offset with brightly colored accessories and accents. The whole space feels homey and warm considering the starkness of the white.

"What do you think?" John asks from the living room. I turn to find him looking out at the view of the city.

"I love it, John. But can I afford this?" I feel like it might be a little too far out of my budget, so I don't want to get my hopes up.

John turns to face me. "Well, it's a little unusual, but since we had been expecting to sponsor you and take care of your move financially and you got ahead of us there, Mr. McAllister is willing to include this apartment in your contract for a year."

"You're kidding me." I stare wide-eyed at him.

"Nope. The place is yours if you want it. And after a year, if you don't want to make other arrangements, you can more than afford it, Charlotte. Trust me."

I'm almost speechless. I scan the space, taking in the details and see myself being very comfortable here. "And there are three bedrooms?" I ask, wondering about the rest of the living space.

"Yes, all furnished. If you want one of the bedrooms converted into a home office we can do that, but I will say that when you leave work, we want you to leave it in the office and not work at home."

I nod, agreeing with that. It will help me not become obsessive about the job if I don't have a dedicated place to work at home. "Which way are the bedrooms?"

John points back toward the entrance hall. "On the right you have the master suite, then on the other side are the other two bedrooms. All en suite of course and then there is a guest bathroom here." He indicates a door on the opposite side of the entrance way.

"There's outside space too. Your balcony runs from the living room, past the kitchen and wraps around to the master suite. All the windows are sliders."

I walk down the hall to the master suite and my mouth drops when I look inside. A huge king size bed takes up one wall, the bedding is white but the frame and headboard are a deep teal and accents in shades of teal all around the place make the room feel inviting and warm. "You have an amazing designer."

"Mr. McAllister likes to make all the design decisions himself."

"Wow. Well for someone I've never met he sure picked out colors I love."

"He has a way of knowing what people like."

I walk over to the window and look out over the place I now call home.

"So?" John prompts behind me.

I spin around with a big smile. "So, when can I move in?"

He grins, reaching into his pocket and handing me a set of keys. "Anytime you are ready."

I cover my mouth with my hand to prevent a squeal of delight escaping when I accept them. "Thank you so much, John."

"Don't thank me." He holds up his hands.

"I'll have to break it to Louise tonight. She won't mind having her place back to herself I'm sure."

My phone buzzes and I look down at the screen, freezing at the sight of his name.

**Rhys:** Thank you, kitten x

I open it up and am hit again with the heady need he makes me feel when I see us together in the picture. Remembering where I am, I guiltily close the message and look up.

"Sorry, John, I didn't mean to be rude."

"No problem, I should get going anyway. Do you want me to leave you up here to look around a little more?"

"If you don't mind. I'll be back down in a little bit."

"Of course, take your time. I'll see you later." He excuses himself and a few seconds later I hear the front door click shut.

This time I don't hold back my squee of excitement. This place is amazing, everything I could have hoped for and more. I can't wait to show Louise and begin snapping pictures with my phone so I can show her later. Taking my time I visit each room, taking in details and peeking into closets and storage spaces, cataloging it all on my phone so I can revisit it from my desk later.

I am in love with this apartment.

Deciding I'm not going to avoid telling Louise, I text her.

**Me:** I have news. Pizza Express tonight?

Buttering her up with her favorite is smart.

**Louise:** Sounds great and intriguing. It's a date.

I smile and set my phone on the kitchen counter so I have free hands to explore all of these cabinets.

My phone buzzes again while I'm investigating the massive refrigerator and I decide it's probably time to stop daydreaming about what it's going to be like living here and get back to work. I pick up my phone and can't help my smile.

**Rhys:** How's your day going?

Well, he's trying.

**Me:** Good. Actually, I just got myself a new place to live!

**Rhys:** That's great news, you should celebrate. Can I take you out?

**Me:** Sorry, I'm having dinner with a friend.

I know exactly how that sounds and I'm not sorry one little bit. I'm already in deep enough shit. Every time he calls me kitten I get giddy and he knows it. It won't hurt for him to think I might have another date.

**Rhys:** Lucky friend. Maybe another night?

Gracious in defeat. Who would have thought it? I decide to reward his good grace.

**Me:** Definitely.

# TWELVE

"I'm going to miss you." Louise mopes while I zip my last suitcase closed. "You're moving into a dream apartment and I am still in this little shithole."

"Hey! This is not a shithole."

"I know. I know."

"It will be good for you and Cami to have your own space."

"Yeah," she sighs with absolutely no enthusiasm at all.

"Come on, Lou, we knew I wouldn't live with you forever." Guilt eats at me because Cami is the main reason it didn't last longer and even though it's the truth, I don't want her to think that.

"You know she probably won't be around as much as you think," Louise reasons, seeing right through me.

"How the hell do you do that?" I ask.

"I can see it in your eyes, you go into panic mode when you go out of your comfort zone."

"Come on now, I think I do a great job of hiding it."

"You do, but I know you." She gives me that knowing smile that I want to smack off her face.

My phone chimes loudly. Since I'm with Louise it can really only be one of two other people.

"Oh you have the sound up on your phone, very interesting." Louise waggles her eyebrows at me.

I feel my face heating. "Shut your mouth."

Louise laughs. "Is it the friend, or the soon to be lover?"

"Louise! You don't know that."

Rhys and I met for coffee once this week, because between work and my move that was all I could fit in. He was a perfect gentleman, I was a bit disappointed. I kinda wanted him to go all alpha on me again. He has been texting though, quite a bit, hence the volume being up on my phone. I get a little thrill of excitement when I hear it...and of course Louise picks up on that detail right away.

"Oh I know, Charlotte, your bright red face is telling me all I need to know. Check your text."

I swipe open my phone quickly and see a message from Rhys.

**Rhys:** Dinner tonight?

"He wants to go to dinner tonight."

"Aren't you a lucky duck. Your stuff from storage is already there, so you only have these few things to move and unpack. You should go."

"I know. I'm going to say yes."

**Me:** Sure, after I'm done moving?

**Rhys:** Need help?

**Me:** No, Louise and I have it. Ttyl

**Rhys:** Okay. Send me your address and a time.

"You deserve to have some fun," Louise tells me, placing her hand on my forearm and squeezing. I know she wants to hug me but she knows my limits and refrains.

"I agree." I nod, because I do, but Louise seems determined to get her message heard and grips my arm a little tighter.

"I mean it. You need to go out there and take some chances, step out of your comfort zone. It's what you intended when you made the move, so you have to see it through. Really Charlotte, a fifteen-minute tube ride is a hell of a lot better than a six hour flight. You could live with me until we're old and gray, but that's not what you need. You need to live." She throws her arms around me and I return the hug, releasing her before she's ready.

"Okay." I nod, not giving her any more than that, then I pull out the handle of my suitcase. "We'd better get going."

---

It takes me less time than I thought to unpack my clothes and then take a quick shower. I'm dressed down and leave my hair tousled and my face free of any makeup. I know it's stupid, but since he literally let my hair down the other night, I've been seeing myself in a new light. He always looks so relaxed and I always look so—me. I feel the need to show him how I look when I'm not being Charlotte the businesswoman. I don't switch her off nearly as often as I should and it's something I need to do more. If that turns him off, better now than later.

I find myself staring down at my phone. I want to text him, I need to text him. But I'm so unsure. Do I want him coming to my place? I don't trust myself this close to a bed with him.

**Me:** Hey.

I'm such an idiot, who says just 'hey'? Dumbass.

**Rhys:** Hey yourself.

**Me:** I'm all finished here. What time are you free?

**Rhys:** I've just been sitting around waiting for your message, kitten. What's your address?

**Me:** How about we meet at St. Paul's?

**Rhys:** Our bench?

I smile at my phone feeling goose bumps scatter across my arms. He remembers where we saw each other outside of the church.

**Me:** Yes, perfect. Say thirty minutes?

**Rhys:** I'll be there.

Twenty minutes later, I reach Festival Gardens and follow the meandering path through the matured trees. I reach the freshly mowed yard to the rear of the cathedral and find that luck is on my side. I can see from here our spot is open. I check the time and still have a few minutes to spare, so I head over to claim the bench before anyone else can. I have a clear view both ways of the path that circles the church, but since I don't know which direction to expect him from, I just people watch.

Without warning, hands come from behind me and cover my eyes. I gasp and tense, ready for a fight or flight situation.

"Hello, kitten."

"Rhys." His name slips out on a sigh and I feel my skin heat with the humiliation of how I sound.

He chuckles and removes his hands from my eyes, brushing his knuckles down my face and tilting my head back. I look up into his grinning up-side-down face and he leans over me pressing a kiss to my lips. I'm flooded with a warm feeling pumping through my veins.

Just as quick he pulls away and comes around to the front of the bench.

Wow. He looks so effortless. Dressed all in distressed black which sets off his ink perfectly, I'm happy I made the considerable effort to dress down. I feel like I don't stand out as much.

Rhys holds out a hand and I take it. He leans in and kisses my cheek when I stand, then looks me over, skimming over my flowing hair with appreciation in his eyes. Score one for the relaxed look.

"What would you like to eat, kitten?"

"I could go for something simple like a burger."

"There's a place right around the corner that's good." He slips his hand in mine and we set off on a stroll through the churchyard and out onto the street. There is something liberating about walking with him and feeling so relaxed, taking our time down a street I'm now used to beating in heels and a pencil skirt, walking at pace with the hustling, bustling business crowd. I feel so free.

He catches me staring down at our joined hands and I feel the need to explain myself. "This is weird, isn't it?"

"What is?" He frowns.

"This." I lift our hands to illustrate my point.

"Why do you say that? It's normal. When two people like each other they show it."

I resist the urge to snort. "I wouldn't know. I haven't dated for a long time." As we approach the restaurant, a recollection hits me. "Oh! I think I've eaten here before. Well, not here, but this chain. Louise, my best friend, took me a couple of years back on a visit. It was amazing."

"I'm glad you think so. It's one of my favorites." Rhys opens the door for me and ushers me inside. We're seated at a booth in a corner, and our drink order is taken. He glances at the menu and sets it aside. "So why haven't you dated?" he asks, casually picking up the conversation I'd hoped was dropped.

I don't need to look at the menu. I order the same type of burger no matter where I go. So I fold my hands on the table and look into the sea of blue open to hearing all my secrets. I just don't know if I want to relive them with him.

"I was too busy running my old company to enjoy anything but seeing it grow and succeed." Each time I say it, it gets a little bit easier to let it go.

"Ahh a workaholic." His eyes are filled with understanding. "I get it."

He chuckles, reaching out to put his hand on mine. "I didn't make it to my thirties, single, by living the party life."

"So you're a workaholic too?" I ask with hope in my words.

"I was," he says simply, and I feel like there is more to that story, but I find I'm more intrigued by his single status.

"So you have never been married?"

He barks out a laugh. "No, and before you ask, I've never been engaged either."

"I wasn't going to ask, but thank you for the information. Unattainable?"

"Not necessarily." His thumb rubs the top of my hand and I have to shut out the scorching sensation it leaves, to hold onto the thread of our conversation.

"You aren't missing much," I say, my tone dry.

"Marriage didn't agree with you?" He raises an eyebrow.

"I'm divorced, so I would have to say it did not." Somehow talking about my marriage doesn't really hurt as much as it did in the beginning.

He holds up both hands. "I don't want to pry."

I tilt my head studying his eyes, they are filled with sincerity and not pity. "You're not prying. I'm an open book."

Thankfully the waiter comes and takes our order, now would be the perfect time to change the subject.

"So you were a workaholic—but you aren't anymore?" I ask the minute the waiter leaves, hoping to take the focus off my failed marriage.

"I used to put work before everything. Family, love, health, happiness. I don't think I even knew what happiness was if it wasn't associated with profit or success."

I raise my eyes heavenward. Thank God. He really does get it.

"Then I had an epiphany," he continues. "And it changed my

way of thinking." He sits back in the booth, a serious look on his face. "Are you still that way?" He now has a slight frown on his face.

"No, that's one of the reasons why I moved here. I wouldn't say I had an epiphany as such. It was more of a gradual awakening. Starting fresh, breaking bad habits and all that," I say with a flair of my hand. "It was time for me to cut ties and find what was missing in my life."

"And what is that, kitten?"

"When I find it, I'll let you know."

Rhys smiles, but it doesn't reach his eyes. "It's important that you do. Life is too short to waste it working your life away."

"Sounds like you learned that lesson the hard way."

"Yeah, I was brought up thinking that money is everything. Build your empire first, my Pop would say. Everything comes to you when you have money."

"I grew up poor and used to think that if I had money everything would be sunshine and rainbows. Now I have money and I find I am still in search of my rainbow, only it's not a pot of gold I want to find at the end."

He raises his glass. "Cheers to that, kitten."

The waiter comes back and places our plates down before us and the conversation as we eat is lighter and flirty. I can't pinpoint exactly what it is about Rhys, but he makes me want him, it's something I can't control. Truth be told it's terrifying. But, I'm sick and tired of always playing it safe. The waiter comes and takes our plates away and Rhys pays the bill quickly and with no fanfare. Normally, I would insist on paying at least my share, but I decide not to fight him. I'm going to pick my battles with Rhys and I have my sights set on something else tonight. The more time I spend with him, the more I want him. It's time I let loose.

He takes my hand and leads me out into the cool evening, turning to face me. "So, kitten, the night is young. What do you fancy doing now?"

"Want to come back to my place?" I blurt before I can change my mind.

# THIRTEEN

He's hard, and it's not something he can even attempt to hide. I mean, I'd already felt him hard against me that night in the alley, but it was dark and surprise obviously had me missing key facts. Tonight I'm not missing any details. We'd just spent the entire elevator ride up to my floor making out like horny high schoolers. Rhys devoured me until we were both breathless.

I don't know what I'm thinking as I lead him to my apartment, I am so out of my depth. But something, raging desire probably, pushes me on. That and the need to get Rhys and his massive hard-on out of the hallway, before any of the neighbors I have yet to meet, come out and get the absolute worst first impression of me imaginable.

The second he closes my front door, I turn and drink him in. With the hard reality of him before me, I switch off the rational part of my brain and go all in, pushing myself against him. I breathe in the heady scent of arousal between us, feeling every inch of the firm body he obviously works hard to maintain, as he walks me backwards to the wall.

"Kiss me," I plead, not recognizing my own voice. This needy creature I'm becoming is completely foreign to me.

"You don't have to ask me twice, kitten." He lifts me, pressing my back to the foyer wall, taking me in a deep and hungry kiss. He groans into my mouth. I'm pinned to the wall by his determination, it's like he can't get close enough to me and he's unapologetic in trying. It feels wonderful and I need more. Greedily I take what he gives, until at last his need for oxygen pulls him away. He tears his lips away gasping. "Fuck, kitten."

I pant as a jolt of desperate excitement flashes through me, striking deep in my core. The need in his eyes and the fevered sound of his voice awaken yet more feelings in me I'm unfamiliar with. I feel proud of myself. Maybe I'll have regrets in the morning, but knowing I've done that to him, made him so hungry for me, it's so intoxicating I don't care about tomorrow. And I can't deny what that name does to me anymore. It makes me wet, pure and simple.

"I like it when you call me that," I whisper, surprised at myself for giving him the satisfaction of the admission. I can't even force my walls to stay in place now that I'm this close.

As he lowers me down, he makes sure to drag every hard inch of himself over me. My breath quickens though, because even through two layers of denim, the sensitive nerves at my center still zing with pleasure at the contact. I need to get him into my bed or I will end up throwing him down on the foyer floor.

"Better get me to your room quick," he growls into my neck, kissing a path down to my exposed collarbone. "I'm fit to have you right here." His voice vibrates straight through me and I feel relieved I'm not the only one who can't wait another second. I grab his hand and lead him down the hall.

He pulls me back toward him even as we make progress, his arms wrapping around my body and his hands roaming blindly over my back, while his tongue seeks mine like it hasn't only been seconds they were apart. We fumble our way toward the bedrooms, bumping and colliding with surfaces, taking far too long about it. In the doorway of my room, his hands slip into my hair, fisting it and pulling my head back slightly so that he can nip and suck at the sensitive skin of my throat. I moan appreciatively.

He slides his hands from my hair and down my back, pausing when he cups my ass, all the while staring at me reverently. Holding his gaze, I skirt my fingers under his shirt, meeting hard ridges of muscle and wondering how far the ink spreads. I pull my eyes from his for a moment, lifting the shirt over his head and letting it drift out of my hand and drop to the floor.

The sight before me makes my mouth water. Hard abs and smooth skin, peppered with works of art I hope to have time to look at later. One tattoo peaks my interest however. Across his chest in large Celtic style script is a word I'm not familiar with and stands out proudly. SAORSA.

I stroke my fingertips lightly across it wondering about its meaning. Before I can even voice my question, Rhys captures my fingers in his, lifting them to his lips and placing a soft kiss on the pads. "It's Gaelic," he tells me.

"What does it mean?"

"There isn't really a word for it in English." He extends my arm, pressing his lips to the inside of my wrist, sending the sensation rippling through my pulse. "It means…" He pauses, thinking. "Finding your salvation, your liberty. It's about finding freedom from the things in life that weigh you down. Redemption from your mistakes. For me it means giving myself permission to be more than just my duties and responsibilities. It's a reminder to live." Rhys touches his chest, over his heart, then shakes his head and looks away.

I touch his cheek, bringing his eyes back to mine.

"It's important to me," he says, sounding embarrassed that

he'd exposed so much of himself. It's the first time I've seen him vulnerable.

I nod, not so much in understanding, more in awe. I never saw Rhys as such a deep soul. I want to know more about him. I want to know everything. But desire is still pulsing inside me, and we'll have time to talk later.

I reach for the hem of my own shirt and whip it over my head. For a second I wish I would have worn something a little sexier but when Rhys rakes his eyes over me, I know it doesn't matter.

"Gorgeous," he murmurs as he brushes his knuckles across my nipple. The only barrier between us is the lace of my bra.

I move to his belt, unbuckling it and pulling it through all the loops, the gleam in his eyes making me bolder than I'd typically be. I toss his belt aside and unbutton the first button on his jeans. I don't manage to get any further because he cages me in with his arms, taking my mouth in a demanding kiss.

Hot. Fuck.

My pants are making my skin itch, too much clothing. I manage to unbutton them and shimmy out without breaking the kiss, eager to have his skin pressed to mine. Wrapping my arms around his neck, his strong arms come around me. His fingers trace my spine all the way down until he slips them into my panties cupping my ass with a firm grip. I break the kiss with a gasp.

"Fuck, Rhys. I need you." He chuckles and squeezes my ass almost to the point of pain but it hurts so good.

"What are you waiting for?" His accent seems thicker in the heat of the moment.

I try to move out of his grasp but he presses his fingers deep into the round flesh of my ass and lifts me. My legs automatically wrap around his waist and I clutch him tighter around the neck as he walks into my room.

I unravel my legs when he reaches the end of the bed, sliding down his body. I gulp with anticipation at the thought of him inside of me. The second my feet hit the floor his fingers go to work, unclasping my bra. He slides the straps off my shoulders and carelessly tosses it aside. He skims his fingers over my nipple, watching mesmerized as it stiffens at his touch. A shiver of pleasure rolls through me when he rolls it between his finger and thumb. I cry out, feeling the tug in the deepest part of me. He licks his lips longingly and before I can even think 'oh god, yes', the warm tug of his tongue is pulling on nerves that run right to my clit. I'm ready to beg for release, but he doesn't give me the chance.

He then pulls away, leaving wet kisses on my stomach, moving slowly down, ever closer to the center of me. His hands, those god damn hands, working magic wherever they touch. My head falls back when he begins to slide my panties down my legs.

"Kitten, look at me," he commands, and I swear I feel his breath there. I shiver with anticipation.

I look down and into his large lustrous eyes. I've never had anyone on their knees before me like this. I've only been with one man and he never—well he never got that look of worship in his eyes—not even in the beginning. It's unnerving, the blaze of intensity, the look of possession. I could freak out, but it's intoxicating. He's looking at me like I'm his and...I want to be.

Slowly he grasps my ankle and lifts my leg, setting it on the end frame of the bed, opening me completely to him. I want to cover myself but I also want to see what comes next.

He leans in, eyes still fixed on mine, and swipes his tongue through my folds and over my clit, sending sparks through every part of me.

"Oh God," I gasp.

His eyes close and he groans. "Fuck, kitten. You taste so good," he murmurs, his eyes re-opening and focusing on what's in front of him for the first time. I feel self-conscious watching on while he parts me with his fingers and studies me, before laving his tongue once again across that knot of nerves. The bliss that action brings however, quickly erases all thought.

He licks and sucks expertly, slipping first one, then two fingers inside me to brush over a place I thought only I knew existed. My legs begin to tremble and I throw my head back, moaning in amazement that it could ever feel so good. He seems to like this reaction because he ups the ante; sucking my clit into his mouth and rolling over and over it with his tongue while his fingers do things inside of me I have never been capable of. I cry out, it's pure heaven. I can't get enough and yet I hope there isn't much more to come because I fear my legs are about to give way.

He doesn't stop, he goes faster, deeper. I climb higher and higher, until at last I reach the peak and my body tenses, giving my legs the strength in the final throes to support me through the most blinding, consuming orgasm I have ever experienced. I cry incoherently, gripped with pleasure so intense it almost hurts.

His fingers sliding out of me is what brings me down from wherever I was flying. The loss of him makes me whimper. I look down to find him gazing up at me reverently, the gloss of his eyes filled with purpose and pleasure. Cradling his face in my hands, I stroke his cheek and he closes his eyes, leaning in to my touch.

I study him. The cut of the muscles on his back carving light and shade amongst the tattoos, his well-worn jeans sitting so low on his hips I see a glimpse of dimples above his firm ass. He's perfect, even though perfection is a contradiction to the look he so artfully has going on. It's all rough and worn, his hair and his ink and the way he dresses make him look hard and wild. It all had me assuming he would be hard and wild in every way. And while I'm sure he could be, nothing about him gave away the idea that he could be so reverent or tender. I hadn't expected worship when I jumped him in the foyer.

My insides clench at their emptiness recalling his fingers there only moments ago and a surge of need has me tugging him upward.

"I can't wait any longer," I plead.

I need to be filled with Rhys. He's in my thoughts, my heart and I need him in my body. I'm losing myself to him and I know it. He chuckles at my impatience but I know he's feeling the same heated rush as he gets to his feet and drops his jeans and boxers in a flash. I gulp as he kicks them aside and his length sways from the motion. How will I take him when it's been so long? Hell even if it had been yesterday, Henry had nothing on him. Rhys is going to be a challenge and while I fear it might break me, I never shy away from a challenge.

I see the hunger in his eyes and prepare for things to turn frantic again, but it doesn't. He's calm as he steps forward, brushing his knuckles tenderly down the side of my face. He's a juxtaposition of untamed passion and control. I lean into his touch then turn and place a kiss on his retreating hand.

"I could spend all night looking at you. You're fucking beautiful," he says, devouring me with his eyes. He trails his knuckles down my body, grazing my nipples and then dipping even lower.

Standing before him completely naked, I feel as beautiful as he says. It's empowering. I take a step closer, bringing my hands up to trace the tattoos that cover his biceps on each side. I follow the lines until I reach his waist, then I sink down on my knees before him, ready to worship him as he worshipped me.

I look up at him and watch as he strokes his hand over his length slowly back and forth. It's mesmerizing. I gaze back up and lick my lips. Rhys groans in appreciation and I open my mouth to him. He guides his head to my waiting tongue and I close my lips around him and swirl my tongue around his head.

"Fuck, kitten," he says between clenched teeth.

I love the power that I have right now, it's a heady feeling controlling his pleasure. He cradles my face and then grips my hair with his other hand, the tight sting on my scalp turning me on even more. He tentatively works himself deeper and I accept as much of him as I can. I pull back and sink down again, taking him a fraction more on each pass. I find my rhythm and work on giving him the kind of pleasure he gave me, when he pulls out suddenly and pulls me to my feet, his hand still twisted in my hair.

He takes my mouth with a searing kiss, his tongue demanding as he works me into a heated flush, then he releases me. I can visibly see his labored breathing.

"Not like this," he breathes. "I want to come while I'm deep inside you."

"Now," I pant. "Please."

He chuckles deep and I swear I feel it in the pit of my belly. I place my hands on his chest and give him a push. He wasn't expecting it, I can tell by the shocked look on his face as he falls back on the bed. I crawl up his body leaving wet kisses as he laughs, pulling me up over him until I'm straddling his hips.

I smile down on him and suck in my lower lip, fuck he's beautiful.

He places a hand on my mound and slightly lifts me, his other hand guides his cock to my opening. I stare down at him, poised at my entrance and look back up at him as he removes his hands and places them on my hips ready to push me down. Despite the lust surging through me, I resist the urge to hurry and have him fill me and instead, slowly sink down on his length.

"Ohh..." I moan as my back arches and my head falls back. My heart is pounding and my body is burning with need. I follow the beat and start to move on him, taking full control of the rhythm and depth. He lets me lead, only guiding my hips to keep my motions fluid and soon I'm lost in the roll of our bodies moving together. Then I feel his legs rise behind me and with a jerk of his hips he is even deeper in me. I close my eyes and cry out loudly.

"Look at me, kitten," he commands gruffly.

I look down at him and he nods his approval. His tattoos dance with their strain, veins popping out as he begins to thrust hard up into me. I'm so close to losing myself, but I fear he's going to finish before I'm able to get there again. I trail my hand down my body. His eyes watch my every move. I press a finger to my clit and moan, but he takes my hand away and I almost sob.

"Your pleasure is mine to give," he growls, thrusting hard. His hand replaces mine and he doesn't let up on his thrusts as he matches his pace with his circling thumb. I shatter into a million pieces around him, my pussy clenching him so hard he curses. His rhythm doesn't falter though and he grabs my hips thrusting harder, deeper, raising his hips up so as be as deep inside me as he can get. His ab muscles strain, glistening with sweat, then I see them twitch and tighten and he follows me into bliss, crying out his curses.

It's beautiful.

He pulls me down so I'm laying on top of him. We're both breathing heavy, trying and failing to catch our breath.

Wow. That is the only thing I can think.

"Wow is right, kitten," he laughs.

Shit, did I say that out loud?

Rhys lifts up off the bed, my legs still wrapped around his waist, his still hard cock pressing between us and stands as if he doesn't have my substantial weight in his arms.

"What are you doing, Rhys?" I don't recognize my own voice, it has a sleepy sultry sound to it.

"Shower," he says simply and carries me into my bathroom and right into the walk-in shower. He lowers me down out of the reach of the jet and turns on the water. I'm a bit off kilter, Henry was never part of the clean up after sex. My arms come up to cover my breasts.

"A little late to be shy, kitten," Rhys says with an amused grin.

My face heats and I make myself lower my arms, looking at him with a challenge in my eyes.

"Good girl," he murmurs, testing the water before dragging me under the spray with him. He takes the soap, lathering it between his strong hands and washes me gently, while I stand dumbfounded letting it happen.

Those words shouldn't have this effect on me, I never thought of myself as the type to relish being called a good girl. I'm a strong woman, not subservient, but there it is. A good girl I must be, because I feel the goose pimples rise on my arms. He pinches a nipple and my eyes close with pleasure.

"Turn," he instructs, his accent thick and sexy. I follow the command.

He washes my back and then pays extra attention to the cheeks of my ass, cleaning everything a little too much. That easily I need him again and I arch into his hand.

"Put your hands up on the wall."

I brace myself as I'm told and he rinses the soap off me, then he urges my stance wider. He steps close and I feel his still hard length resting between the round globes of my ass and I groan.

"You're so fucking beautiful." His breath on my neck makes me shiver even in the steaming shower. He places an open kiss where my shoulder and neck meet, as his hand dives between my legs. His other hand comes around me and cups my breast, while his fingers drive me fucking crazy between my legs.

He pulls back for a second and then his cock fills me with one thrust.

Heaven, that's where he's taking me to. He wraps his arms around me, his chest flush with my back. His hips keep thrusting, taking me higher and higher.

My senses are in overload. I try to stand straighter, to turn maybe? Something, anything to slow down this out of control ride I'm taking before I die from pleasure. But he holds me in place. Then he plays dirty and presses a finger to my clit, whispering, "Fly, kitten."

Thank fuck he's holding me up, because I come immediately. So hard that I think I black out for a second. He groans into my ear as he too reaches his release.

I'm spent. Ruined even. My boneless legs can't fully support me any more than my addled brain can feel ashamed of the fact. How he is still standing is beyond me. Clearly sexual stamina is something you have to work at because I am out of shape and he... yeah, I'm not going to wonder how often he 'works out'. I just let him wash me again and come down from my high as gracefully as I can manage.

After drying me off, Rhys lifts me and carries me back into the bedroom and lays me down. I begin to worry when he crawls toward me, but relax when he simply wraps me in his arms. I'm going to need a little sleep before I can handle him again. He strokes me lazily and I can feel his body relax against mine. I don't think it will be long before sleep takes us both. I'm drifting off when the buzzing of a cell phone breaks the silence.

"That's not mine," I grumble. "Mine's on silent and abandoned in my purse out by the front door."

He kisses my shoulder. "You were in a hurry to get me in bed."

"I wasn't alone in that endeavor." I turn in his arms and look at him. "Are you going to answer that?"

He shakes his head. "Too comfy. They can leave a message. It will stop in a second."

The buzzing stops.

"See?" He nods in satisfaction.

It promptly starts back up.

"See?" I fire back with a smirk.

"Shit," he curses and unwraps himself from me. "Sorry, I'll take care of it." He walks naked and unashamed across the room and digs the phone out of his pants. "Yes?" he barks into the phone.

Laying on my side, my head propped up on my arm, I watch his back stiffen.

"I've already told you—" he begins, obviously cut off by whoever is on the other end. "That's not my problem." There is a long pause, before he rakes his fingers through his hair. "Mother-fucker!" he snarls and looks at the screen of his phone before snatching up his jeans.

He turns toward me, buttoning them quickly. He didn't even put his boxers on first. The light from the bathroom show the firm lines on his face. "I have to go."

"Oh." I swallow, sitting up with the sheet held to my chest. "Okay..."

"I'm sorry, something came up. It won't take long. I can come back." He says it more as a question than a statement.

I frown, the regrets I worried about having all rearing their ugly heads at once. "I'm really tired, I'll probably be asleep. Don't trouble yourself. I'll uhhh see you around."

He reaches the side of the bed with two long strides and sits down. "This isn't the way I wanted to end our night together, kitten. Leave the door unlocked and I will be back." He doesn't wait for me to reply. He leans in and steals a kiss, then cursing he breaks away and rushes out the door.

The second I hear the click of the front door I throw off the sheets. Yanking a shirt over my head, I stomp down the hall. What was I thinking? The soreness between my legs reminds me that I wasn't thinking. I let him in and he made me lose my head. The man just fucked me twice and ran out the door. Nice, real nice. I go directly to the front door and lock it. Then I turn off all the lights and march back to bed.

My heart is beating so loud I can hear it pounding in my ears.

It's about an hour after he left that I hear the door handle turn. It rattles a little, then he softly knocks. I hold my breath, afraid he will know I'm awake.

"Charlotte?" His voice is muffled but I can tell he's being quiet so he doesn't wake the neighbors. Which is perfect because I can say I didn't hear him.

I bite the sheets to keep from calling back. The temptation to have him back in my bed even though he ran out on me is too strong and I am too weak.

He curses then I hear his hand slide down the door, and then...silence.

As tired as I am, I don't fall back to sleep. I'm too angry and too sad. Because no matter what he says tomorrow, I know the voice on the other end of the phone was female and I'd bet my last dollar I know who it was.

## FOURTEEN

I arrive at my desk the next morning to find a sticky note stuck to my keyboard. New login details for the system. I frown, picking it up and heading back out to Jo's desk.

"What's this?"

"We've all got them." She holds up hers to prove it. "Some kind of huge security breech last night. IT wiped all login rights and had to issue new ones. I don't know any more than that, sorry. Oh," she says as an afterthought. "They said we should change them, but it can't be the same as your past login."

"Great," I mumble. "I'd only just memorized that one."

"I know, it sucks."

I return to my office, sticking the note to my desk until I have a chance to get on and personalize my ID, then I hang my purse on the hook and take my notebook and phone out.

I notice another message from Rhys. The third since I woke up.

The first was another apology for running out on me last night and letting me know that he did try to come back, but I must have been asleep because he knocked and I didn't let him in.

The second followed thirty minutes later, where, after no reply to the first, he simply ignored my silence and cheerfully asked if he could cook me dinner tonight.

Now it's just three words. "Ignoring me, kitten?" Three innocuous words which should irritate me further, but instead have me imagining the kind of punishment a man like him might concoct for such a crime. Sweet Jesus, do I have no willpower? He fucked the sense out of me, then only minutes later he goes running back to Lisa the moment she demands. And here I am trying to ease the aches he left both between my legs and in my chest. Pathetic, Charlotte. Completely pathetic.

The click clack of Jo's shoes alerts me that she is two seconds away from entering my office. I silently thank her for her arrival, I need the distraction, before I'm tempted to answer him. Or worse.

"Charlotte?" she says, nudging in through the partially open door.

"Come on in."

She's carrying a heavy looking file box and she uses her foot to kick the door shut as she crosses the room.

"Here are the files you wanted printed. It's all here. Everything back to 2014," she huffs and drops it onto my desk.

"Holy crap."

"I know, I worked up quite a sweat in the copy room yesterday." She wipes her brow. "Are you sure you're doing the right thing?" she asks nervously.

"Yes, if I don't present all these documents to Mr. McAllister so he can see the full extent, then I am not doing the job he pays me for. What he chooses to do about it is on him."

"Okay." She nods. "In that case, I've checked with Mr. Tesi's assistant and she confirmed that Mr. McAllister has a meeting with Mr. Tesi in the conference room at ten. If you want to barge in, that's your chance."

I glance at the clock on my office wall, I have thirty minutes to prepare. "Thank you, Jo. For everything."

"No problem. Is there anything else?"

"Not right now."

"Just buzz me if you need me." She opens the door and returns to work.

I stare at the box. Proof of every penny that Elisabeth King stole from the company during her employment here. I plan on crashing their meeting because Mr. McAllister is an ocean wave. I can't pin him down. I have a hunch that his elusiveness has something to do with what he knows I've found in the finances. Maybe he's embarrassed that it's obvious he was banging her and she was stealing from him? Whatever his reasons, it isn't going to go away unless he sees how real this is. I'm afraid he will just keep on ignoring the problem. I just hope I still have a job after such a rude introduction.

I breathe to calm myself and without giving myself permission, I look at my phone again. Nothing more from Rhys. I decide to text my confidant, Michael. I feel like I have so much to fill him in on today, but I can do that later. I just want to tell someone I'm potentially about to get myself fired and since he has supported me through the whole thing, it seems right that it's him.

**Me:** I'm crashing McAllister's ten o'clock. I may get fired. Wish me luck.

He doesn't reply, but he's working so that's to be expected. I just wanted to share. Knowing he will root for me when he reads it is all the encouragement I need. Now I just need to get prepared for the show.

Thirty minutes later, I gather the files and place the lid back on the box, holding my head high as I march out of my office and along to the conference room. I never wanted this to be the subject of our first meeting and I'm concerned for the impression I'm about to make, but hopefully he can look past the abrupt entrance I'm about to make and see that I'm actually not just the new pushy American. I'm great at my job and I've put an end to him being screwed out of so much money.

I stalk down the corridor. He should worry less about his first impression of me and more about what kind of leader he's coming off as. I've been here long enough that I am starting to wonder how much he even cares about this company. I was given the impression that the owner was an active partner, who took the role seriously, but I have yet to see evidence of that.

Maybe I won't give him the chance to fire me, if it comes to it, maybe I'll quit.

Squaring my shoulders, I reach the conference room and find the door open and no one around. I stand staring in disbelief at the empty space. What is going on with this guy? I know they should be here right now, it's on both of their schedules. Determined now to get to the root of the issue, I turn on my heel and head for John's office. I march past his assistant, box still in hand and reach out my knuckle to knock sharply on his door.

"Come in," he calls.

I use my elbow to open the handle and step in with confident strides, only to halt in place when I'm greeted with just John, alone. His sleeves are rolled up and he is behind a mountain of paperwork.

"Charlotte," he says in surprise at my entrance. "Everything okay?"

"I—" I stammer, so confused by the situation I don't know where to begin. "I thought you were meeting with Mr. McAllister at ten?"

"I was," he confirmed, sounding just as confused. "He called in about twenty minutes ago to cancel. He had a personal matter to attend to first thing that couldn't wait. Said he would drop by later."

"I see..." I stare at John, my temper deflating. I was so psyched to finally get this over with, I don't know which way to turn now.

"Was there something I can help you with?" he asks tentatively.

I sigh, dropping the box into one of the chairs in front of his desk, then taking the other for myself. "I was hoping to crash your meeting."

"Oh?"

I pinch the bridge of my nose and think how best to phrase my thoughts. "Don't you think my game of cat and mouse with Mr. McAllister has gone on long enough?"

John frowns. "It is unusual that he hasn't been around much since you started. But he has been a busy man of late and he trusts his staff."

"He trusts them a little too much in my opinion." I point at the box on the chair to my right.

"What pray tell is that?" he asks.

"That," I jab a finger at it. "Is a record of everything that this Elisabeth King bought or withdrew on Liberty's dime."

He scowls and gets to his feet, coming around the desk. Without a word he lifts the top off the box and whistles when he sees the scale of the problem. Thousands of pages make up the records I pulled from the system, documenting every single transaction connected to ELISKIN that has no supporting documentation. Even if we give her the benefit of the doubt and assume some of them are accounting errors or sloppy record keeping, we are still looking at seven figures here.

He lifts a sheet from the top and inspects row after row of figures. His brows raise higher and higher as he reads down the page.

"I've been trying to tell you that her embezzlement was quite extensive."

"Jesus." He runs his hands through his hair in an unusual show of stress.

"Do you think we can get him to show his face now? John, we are talking millions, this could break a company. We are lucky that Liberty is profitable. But this has still come right out of the profit margin."

"I will talk to him as soon as he gets back."

"Good, I think we should get the authorities involved as soon as possible." I stand and pace the space in front of his desk.

"I don't know if he will agree to that."

I face him, taking a step toward the desk and brace my hands on it. "What do you mean? Was he so in love with her that her stealing millions from him is okay?" I take a few deep breaths and force myself to sit back down.

"I understand your frustration. We can only advise him. The ultimate decision is his."

I let out another breath. "I'm sorry, John. I know my place. I would just handle this very different if I was in his position."

"We both would. But there are other factors at play here. One of Liberty's biggest customers and a personal friend of Mr. McAllister is Elisabeth's father."

"Shit."

"Exactly."

"Okay," I huff. "I'll leave it with you to set up the meeting." I stand and look at him as he studies another sheet from the box. "But John, I want in on the meeting."

"You'll be there, you have my word."

"Thank you." I nod, leaving him to digest it all.

I cross the main office to my area and notice Jo's absence as I pass her desk, hoping against hope she's on a coffee run, because Lord knows I need something to get me through this day. I close my door behind me and lean against it, dropping my head back to the wood.

"Rough morning, kitten?"

I jump out of my skin and turn to see Rhys sitting on the sofa with his legs crossed.

"You scared the crap out of me." I put a hand to my chest, feeling my heart pounding.

He smirks, but doesn't move. "You've been avoiding me."

"I've been busy," I snap. He's right I have, but I won't admit that to anyone but myself.

"Mmhmm."

"How did you know where I worked?" I scrunch my brows trying to think when I might have told him.

He chuckles and reaches in to his breast pocket, producing a Liberty business card. My Liberty business card.

"Where did you get that?" I demand.

"I swiped it from your hall table when I left last night. Something told me I would need to come hunt you down eventually."

He slowly unfolds his legs and sits up, and that's when I notice what he's wearing. My mouth goes dry at the sight of him. He's dressed in a perfectly tailored suit, wearing it as if he was born to look suave, when I've only seen him in worn black jeans and biker boots. The contrast is staggering. The glimpses of ink on his neck and hands, set against the crisp white of his shirt. His expertly tied double Windsor. I look him up and down, not believing my eyes.

If I hadn't seen for myself what lives and breathes under that suit, I would never believe it. My face heats at the recollection of him last night, hard and wild, moving beneath me until we both found our release. He is to die for, the suit is just the cherry on a delectable cake. And I'm meant to be mad at him. Shit.

It's too late to take back the thorough visual molestation I've just performed. He looks too smug to have not noticed. I look away, annoyed with myself. Damn him.

"Don't stop now, kitten. I was enjoying that," he says, holding open his arms, presumably so I can get a better view.

"What are you doing here?"

"I came to see you," he says, moving toward me.

I take a step toward my desk hoping to put some furniture between us to protect me from my lack of sense when it comes to this man. I wipe my palms down the sides of my skirt and swallow hard.

"You can't shut me out if I'm here." He raises a brow in challenge. "The question is, why are you shutting me out?"

I try to play it cool and shrug. "I've been busy this morning. I would have gotten around to your texts."

"I wasn't talking about the texts. I told you I'd come back last night and when I did, your door was locked and you didn't answer." He takes a step closer to me and I take another one back toward my desk. "So why, kitten?" He advances again and I find I can't move any further when I feel the desk press into the bottom of my butt.

"I was tired and I figured you wouldn't come back. I didn't want to sleep with the apartment unsecured."

"Liar." He is just a breath away from me, his scent surrounds me and I have to fight not to close my eyes and inhale deeply.

He brushes his knuckles down the side of my face. I have to hold myself still as the desire to lean into his touch is overwhelming. I gulp. I am a shitty liar, I know that. I was relying on him barely knowing me, but I guess that failed.

"I didn't think you'd be back," I admit.

"I'm a man of my word," he counters.

I glare at him. "Maybe I didn't want you to come back."

A small smirk curls his lips. "Now we're getting somewhere."

I can't keep a lid on my irritation when I see his satisfaction. "Why would I want you to come back when you have the gall to answer a booty call, fresh from my bed?"

He stifles a laugh. "A booty call?"

I close my eyes and breathe through the desire to wile the smile from his face. "Yes, Rhys, a booty call. You know? Those times when your fuck buddy calls and you go running?"

"I know what a booty call is, kitten. I'm just trying to ascertain how you thought I got one last night." He leans in, his voice too soft for this conversation.

"Because I know that was Lisa calling and you couldn't get to her fast enough." I shove at his shoulder lightly, just trying to get myself some breathing space.

He straightens, turning to sit beside me on my desk. "That was Lisa on the phone. But it wasn't a booty call."

I scoff.

"We haven't had that kind of relationship in a while."

"What difference does it make? She can still call you and you go running to her. That's a problem, Rhys."

"She can't. Last night was—different."

I shake my head. "It's all the same to me. You got out of my bed and went to her. That's all I need to know about where I stand in all of this."

He turns to me and takes my hand. I try to snatch it away, but he holds it between both of his.

"Last night, Lisa had a breakdown. She called me, and yes, I left you, but I didn't go to her."

I look up into his eyes for the first time and frown at the sincerity. "Then where did you go?"

He huffs. "She'd let herself in to my place and was having a meltdown. Worse than any she's had before. She has problems.

Substance abuse, various addictions. I've tried to help her, but this was new. It was time to deal with it properly. So when I left you, I called her father. He met me at my place and I let him in to deal with her. He's going to get her some help. Rehab I hope, but it's not my problem." He squeezes my hand to check I'm following him and I look up, not knowing what to say.

"She'd made quite a mess having her tantrum. It took me a little while to put things right and then I had to get security to change the entry codes and a few other things. Then I came right back to you. I didn't even see her, Charlotte. I'm done." He lifts my chin with a finger. "I'm not her fuck buddy anymore, kitten. Not since I met you."

I blink at him, unsure of what I'm supposed to say to that. Is he trying to tell me that he ended things with Lisa because he met me?

"I wish it hadn't ended how it did, but last night was incredible."

"It was nice," I agree, meekly.

His brows raise. "Just nice?"

His outraged expression makes a giggle erupt from me and I give in. "Okay, you win. It was fucking amazing and to be honest, that scares the shit out of me." I can't look at him as I admit my weakness.

He's having none of it. He lifts my chin and gives me a knowing smile then leans forward and places a chaste kiss on my lips. Even the simple touch of our lips sends lightning bolts through me.

He lingers in my space. "Do you feel that?"

"I do," I whisper. I fist my hands in the lapels of his jacket. I need to shake myself out of his spell. "Why are you in a suit?"

There is a glint in his eyes and they crinkle at the corners. "I had a meeting. Are you trying to change the subject?"

"Yes. You look good in a suit."

"Thank you. Are you going to let me back in?" He smiles. I can tell he's enjoying the back and forth.

"Maybe."

"Maybe isn't good enough, kitten."

"I haven't had a relationship in years. I wasn't very good at the one I had. I—" He cuts me off with a searing kiss. My argument falls flat as I melt for him.

When our lips part, he stands, stepping between my legs in a fluid motion. I'm forced to lean back slightly, bracing myself on the desk and he leans over me, caging me in.

"Don't you think this, thing between us is moving too fast?"

"Kitten, sometimes you just know from the moment you meet someone, that they're special."

His words have warmth spreading through me, softening me to his advance. I can't deny he's right, from the moment I laid eyes on him something in me awoke. Something that had never been awoken before. "I don't understand how you're taking this so easy. Shouldn't you be running for the hills?"

He chuckles. "I live life to the fullest, kitten. I never run from an opportunity."

I feel myself deflate. "So what you're saying is, this happens to you all the time." God I'm an idiot. Of course it does. The way women must look at him as he strolls confidently through life like some Scottish playboy wet dream, he probably has moments like that on the daily. I place a hand on his chest and push him back a little.

"That is not what I said." He takes my hand off his chest and brings it up to his lips, kissing the tips of my fingers.

"Stop that, I can't think when your mouth is on me." I try tugging my hand away, but he holds firm.

"Ever since I met you in the airport, I haven't been able to get you out of my head. It's daunting, but I'd like to see where it's headed, wouldn't you?"

I nod. It's involuntary, as if my body isn't going to allow my brain to screw this up for us and I thank it, because my brain still says run, hide, save yourself. But my body answers his call as he leans over me and teases my lips open with his. We sink into a bone melting kiss. The kind that finishes a conversation without words. I tell him I'm afraid and he says I have nothing to fear. I'm alive with feeling, the brush of his pants on my inner thigh has me opening more to him. As the kiss turns from something cerebral to something altogether more carnal, I'm taken away from my surroundings to a place where only feeling his touch matters.

My cell phone ringing brings me crashing back to my desk. My desk in my office, in my place of work. Oh Jesus. We sever the kiss and share a look of, 'damn, we got a little carried away there', but the cause of the interruption keeps ringing and we both glance at it on the desk beside us.

Michael's name fills the screen and I cringe.

The ringing persists.

"Aren't you going to get that?" he asks with an edge to his voice.

Reluctantly I reach for the phone, accepting the call. "Hey Michael," I greet. "Can I call you back later?"

He doesn't give me an inch his body still pressed against mine, but his face pulls back enough to watch me.

"Sure, I was just checking you were okay and still employed," Michael says.

"I'm all good, I'll fill you in later." Even I can hear the discomfort in my tone.

"Okay. Are we still on for dinner?"

I look at Rhys and cringe as I reply, "Yep, I'll see you tonight."

We end the call, Michael I'm sure wondering why I sounded off and Rhys glowering, with a flash of something threatening in his eyes.

"Who is Michael?" he asks in a strangely calm way.

"He's a friend of mine."

"Friend?"

I cock my head to the side. "Are you jealous?"

"I don't share," he replies, unapologetically.

"That would imply I'm yours to share," I counter, his jealousy giving me a confidence I was sorely lacking only moments ago.

Rhys closes his eyes and takes a breath. "I thought we were just in the middle of establishing that when we were interrupted." He shoots a glare at the phone as if it could somehow convey to Michael his displeasure.

I raise my brows. "I have to say this possessive side of you is pretty hot."

He puts an arm around my waist bringing me closer to him and I wrap my legs around him, feeling him hard between us. "Don't play with fire, kitten."

"Maybe I like the heat."

He growls. "I'm going to make myself crystal clear. I won't share you and I'm not ready to let you go. So you call back this 'friend' and you cancel dinner tonight."

I suppress a laugh, because Mr. Growly doesn't seem in a very giggly place right now, but I'm enjoying his reaction, no lie. "Rhys, I can assure you he's just a friend, nothing more."

"You're a beautiful woman, Charlotte. I highly doubt he doesn't notice that."

"It's not like that between us."

Rhys' phone makes an alert sound from his pocket and he sighs. "Fuck, I have to go." He takes me in a fierce kiss, it's a claim and I love how it feels. "Christ, I could get lost in you right now."

"Why don't you?" I purr, not wanting him to leave.

"I've got a meeting." He breaks contact with me and steps back so we aren't touching.

"I'll meet you here for lunch tomorrow." He smiles and wiggles his brows. "Don't wear knickers." Before I can respond, he smashes his lips down on mine and devours me, before breaking away with a groan. "Cancel your dinner tonight, kitten," he warns, before adjusting himself and taking long strides out of my office.

I take a deep breath and answer, "No" to the empty room.

# FIFTEEN

**Louise:** Got plans tonight? I could use some Charlotte time. x

**Me:** Are you okay?

**Louise:** Yeah, just missing you and want to fill you in on my new single status.

**Me:** Oh shit. What happened?

**Louise:** Nothing really, it just wasn't working out. I'll tell you all about it when I see you. What time do you get off?

I stare at my phone. I haven't cancelled my dinner with Michael as Rhys demanded, I didn't see why I should. Besides, it's not like he would know and what he doesn't know won't hurt him. But if Louise needs me, that's more important. Michael will understand.

**Me:** In a few minutes, but I was meeting Michael for dinner. I'm sure he won't mind if I cancel.

**Louise:** Michael? I thought you were seeing Rhys now?

I roll my eyes.

**Me:** That is yet to be decided.

**Louise:** I see. Don't cancel though, it's fine, I'll see you tomorrow maybe?

Thinking about it, I'm sure Michael wouldn't mind if Louise tagged along.

**Me:** Why don't you join us? You never got to try the food at his brother's restaurant and it is amazing.

**Louise:** I am not crashing your date!

**Me:** It's not a date. It's dinner with a friend and he will be fine about it being two friends I'm sure.

**Louise:** I'll be a third wheel. Honestly, I'll be fine, you go.

**Me:** Nope, I'm not taking no for an answer. Get your butt on a train and meet me there at seven. I'm going to finish up here and go shower. I'll see you soon.

**Louise:** I feel a little bad, but it does sound great. LOL! I'll see you soon. Love you.

**Me:** Love you too.

I decide it's only fair to warn Michael about Louise, so I pull up a text to him.

**Me:** Hey, Louise and Cami broke up and she sounds a little down. Would you mind if she joins us for dinner?

**Michael:** That explains a few work related events today! Of course I don't mind. We can reschedule if you need to be with her.

**Me:** No, I think she's in a good place, but she could just do with a night out, if you don't mind the extra company.

**Michael:** It will be my pleasure. Connor will think I've turned in to some kind of playboy.

**Me:** LMAO! I'll see you later.

---

I stroll into the restaurant a few minutes early and spot Connor taking an order. He winks at me and nods to the back, letting me know to go on ahead. I find Michael staring into his beer so I clear my throat. He jumps and looks up seeming dazed.

"Hey." He smiles, getting to his feet and placing a fond and familiar kiss on my cheek.

"You were miles away. Rough day?"

"You could say that," he says with a grimace.

"Uh oh." I take the seat opposite him and wait for him to sit down and tell me all about it.

"Let's just say, Cami is bad enough on a good day. I was beginning to think she had been possessed by the purest form of evil, but if Louise broke up with her that would explain everything."

I wince. "Damn, that must have been the day from hell."

"A day in hell would have been a welcome change to the day I've had. What happened between them?" He looks utterly shell shocked.

"No idea. Hopefully she will feel up to filling us in when she gets here." I reach over and place a reassuring hand over his. "It's over now. You are safe with me."

He turns his hand over to hold mine and smiles. "I don't know what I'd do without you."

A throat clears beside us and I look up into the thunderous gaze of Rhys. Still wearing his to die for suit from earlier, he looks every bit the suave businessman with a wild edge, only now he looks deadly too.

"Rhys," I gasp, sounding far too guilty for my liking. I pull my hand away from Michael and straighten. I have nothing to hide, but this doesn't look good. I can admit that. "What are you doing here?"

Rhys doesn't reply, he just looks at Michael and then back to me, with his jaw set tight.

Reading the situation perfectly, Michael places his napkin on the table. "I'll just give you two a few minutes," he says, getting to his feet.

Rhys continues to glare at me as Michael excuses himself to a safe distance. He lingers though, to make sure I'm okay, I can see him in my peripheral.

Rhys sits beside me in the booth and I wait.

"I thought I told you I won't share you."

"You did," I reply, simply.

"And I know I told you to cancel your dinner tonight."

"And I told you Michael is just a friend."

"A 'friend' who has had his lips on you," Rhys spits, his hand smacking the table to mark his irritation.

"What?" I scowl. I mean, I can't exactly deny it, but no one knows about that little exception to our otherwise platonic relationship.

"Cut the crap, Charlotte, I've seen the two of you kissing. Outside this very restaurant in fact."

"How?" It's not the defense I probably should be mounting right now, but it's something I want to know.

"I have eyes, I saw him touch you."

"I mean how did you see? There was no one around."

Rhys scoffs. "Well at least you aren't denying it. I was in my car with—" He shakes his head and then it dawns on me exactly who he had been with.

"Lisa," I supply. We had seen her that night and then I do remember a car speeding away.

"It makes no difference. You lied to me."

"I haven't lied to anyone. Michael is my friend. What you saw was us confirming that."

"Friends don't kiss on the street."

"Maybe not," I agree. "But we'd been out twice and felt nothing for each other. We decided we would be better as friends and then before we parted ways for the evening, we tested the water, to make perfectly sure there was no spark. And there wasn't."

Rhys makes a sound of disbelief. "You don't expect me to believe that do you?"

I shake my head in disappointment. "Did you see anything more than a quick and distinctly cool kiss? Hmm?"

"I saw all I needed to see."

"No, Rhys. You saw all you wanted to see," I fire back. "Did you see him pull me into an alleyway and slam me against a wall, kissing me so deeply I forgot who I was?"

Rhys tenses beside me and looks ready to kill. "No."

"No. You didn't. That's what happened when you kissed me, remember? Think about it. If there was anything between Michael and I, don't you think that would have shown itself then? What happened when you kissed me was pure passion and desire and promise. I may have been trying to deny it then, but it was inevitable it would lead us here because neither of us could fight it for long. What happened when Michael kissed me was that we both felt nothing, chalked it up to a failed experiment and carried on our separate ways home.

"We are just friends and that is all we will ever be. But he is my first new friend here and I'm not going to let you tell me I can't see him, however much I want you." I stiffen, knowing this could be make or break for us. I will not be dictated to. "So decide, Rhys. Do you trust me, or are you going to throw this away over a friendship you don't like the idea of?"

"Sorry I'm late..." Louise pants, quickly trailing off when she takes in the scene at the table. The looks she shoots me says everything at once. It says, 'I thought we were meeting the American not the Scottish dreamboat', as well as 'Holy fucking shit, he looks good in a suit, Char!' and a very obvious, 'If you don't want him I could think of a few uses for him'. I'm relieved to see her because she proves to Rhys this was not a date, however I pray he can't read her as well as I can.

Michael comes back over now that there is a neutral party at the table and offers me a supportive smile before turning to Louise. "Louise, right?" He grins. "Good to see you again." He leans in to give her a polite kiss on the cheek in greeting and Louise reciprocates.

"You too, Michael."

They both glance back at us in a moment of silence. Rhys has a decision to make. He stands and I reach across and take a long swig of Michael's beer because I need something to get me through this.

"We haven't been properly introduced," he says, his tone in another realm to the one he was using seconds ago and his entire demeanor more calm. "I'm Rhys, Charlotte's boyfriend."

I choke on the beer.

They all turn to look at me and I wipe at my mouth with the back of my hand.

Rhys' eyes hold a challenge. Daring me to tell them he's wrong.

Louise is WTF-ing with her eyes big time.

Michael looks amused and has a vague look of I-told-you-so about him.

He is first to accept the introduction. "Michael," he says, shaking Rhys' outstretched hand and smiling warmly. "Good to finally meet you, Rhys."

I could kiss him for that. Making sure Rhys knows I've been talking to Michael about him. Which I have. I text Michael every day. I've been telling him more than I've told Louise, but only because she has been caught up in her own stuff lately. Michael is completely up to date except for the boyfriend part, that was news to even me.

"And you must be Louise?" Rhys asks, encouraging Louise out of her WTF-athon.

"That's me," she replies and accepts the kiss to her cheek while glaring at me over his shoulder.

Rhys catches sight of something, or someone across the restaurant and sighs. "I'm so sorry, I have to run. I'm meeting someone and they just arrived." He turns to Louise and Michael. "It was good to meet, I hope I can stay for longer next time. Have a great dinner." Then he turns to me, the thunder previously darkening his face now something lustier. He places a hand on the table and leans in to the booth and just before his lips meet mine, I recognize it for what it is: possessiveness. He kisses me deeply, indecently considering our surroundings, but he's marking his territory so he clearly doesn't care. He wants them to know that what he said is true. We are an item.

He pulls back and smirks. "I'll be back once my meeting finishes, kitten. I can see you home." He winks, then stands and just like that, he leaves. We all watch him walk away in stunned silence and I turn in my seat to make sure I catch a glimpse of who he's meeting. Not that I think it would be Lisa, but I just need to see it for myself.

An older man approaches him and they shake hands warmly, Rhys receiving a pat on the shoulder in a fatherly gesture before they take their seats.

I turn back, satisfied, and face the gaping faces of my friends.

I roll my eyes. "Yes, yes, sit down will you. You're both catching flies."

Michael hands Louise into the seat beside me and reclaims his own. Louise turns to face me and boxed in like this, I feel like I'm facing a firing squad.

"Start talking," she demands.

"I don't know where to start," I admit.

"Start with how you have a boyfriend and I'm just finding out about it now."

Michael almost laughs, but styles it out as a cough. I shoot him a look for not helping me.

"Can we get some drinks first please?" I plead.

Louise looks over her shoulder and calls out loudly to Connor who happens to be passing by, rushing to the kitchen because it's really busy tonight. "Excuse me," she bellows. "We'd like to order some drinks when you're ready."

"Louise!" I admonish.

"What? We need drinks so we can get you talking. I'm just speeding things up."

Connor turns toward the interruption to his kitchen mission, frowning and then smiles impishly when he realizes it's our table that the pain in the ass is calling out from. Without missing a step, he reaches into his apron pocket and fishes out his pen and a small order pad and tosses it on the table.

Louise pulls back and frowns at it, casting a disapproving look at Connor's retreating back. "Rude!" she exclaims.

"Oh relax would you. That's Michael's brother, remember? You met him when you were interfering in my love life," I explain as Michael collects the pad and writes down his beer order and waits for ours.

"Still," she grumbles.

"Don't mind him, he has some manners hidden in there somewhere," he chuckles. "What can I get you ladies?"

"Martini, dirty," I reply in a clipped tone. "Please."

"Sounds good, I'll have the same," Louise adds. "Now spill," she demands as she turns her attention to me.

"Louise, what has gotten into you?"

"I just want to know how my best friend is at boyfriend level with someone and hasn't told me."

"Like when I showed up here to meet your girlfriend?" I ask. "And if you must know, I just found out myself."

"What in the hell does that mean?"

"It means we hadn't really discussed it and now it seems like it's official."

Louise's eyes go wide. "Well why haven't you discussed it?" Her frustration with me is reaching epic levels.

I blush, I can feel it. "There hasn't been much time for discussion."

"Ohhhh!" She leans in. "Tell us more."

I swear Cami must have rubbed off on her, because she is all over the place tonight.

"There is nothing to tell."

"Bullshit!" she cries.

Michael leans back, clearly enjoying our little volley.

"Ugh. We went out last night, we had a very nice evening and I saw him briefly today where we had a conversation about exclusivity and such."

"So you did have time for a conversation."

"Yes, but I hadn't realized it had resulted in a 'we are boyfriend and girlfriend' agreement."

"How can you have a conversation and not realize?" she asks.

"It was more of an 'I don't want you seeing anyone else' conversation," I admit.

"And how do you feel about it?" she urges.

I think for a moment. Despite the surprise, I liked it, a lot.

"Pretty good," I reply. "He kind of surprised me just coming out with it like that. Aren't men supposed to be skittish about commitment? Or have I just been off the scene too long?"

Michael outright laughs. "I'm no expert by any means, but I think that stereotype is about twenty years out of date."

"Oh well. We basically agreed today that we weren't going to see other people, so I guess that means we are an item, right? Him announcing it is what surprised me."

"If you want my opinion," Michael offers. "That part was a pissing contest. He wanted to make sure I knew you were out of bounds."

I can feel my face fall. "Oh God. Do you think he only said it to warn you off? Maybe he didn't really mean it." The level of disappointment I feel really shocks me. I start to panic, I knew I shouldn't have let him in.

"No way, Charlotte. He meant it. He's totally into you, that much is obvious. I just think he went all out and put a label on it tonight to stake his claim. You have nothing to worry about there I assure you."

"He did want me to cancel on you tonight. I think he's a little possessive," I tell him. "It's kinda hot."

"That explains the anger when he found us holding hands." Michael chuckles.

"You two were holding hands?" Louise barks.

"Yeah, all perfectly innocent," I tell her. Then a thought occurs to me. "You don't think he came here tonight to check up on me do you?"

"Did you tell him where you were going?" Louise asks.

"I don't think so."

"Let me go and put this drink order in and I'll check the booking sheet to see when he made the booking."

Michael leaves us and I find myself under the intense scrutiny of my best friend.

"So?" she demands.

"So...?"

"Oh for fuck's sake, Charlotte. So, has he rocked your world? Did the earth move?" She makes a rolling motion with her hand to encourage me to give her information.

"I had a lovely evening with him, that's all there is to say."

"Oh my God," she mutters in frustration. "I have had a really hard weekend. I am this close." She indicates about a quarter inch with her thumb and finger. "To losing my shit with everyone and everything, so please, just give me something, anything. I just want to hear that someone's life doesn't suck as much as mine does right now. Okay?"

I look at her feeling sympathy I know will piss her off.

"Don't look at me that way, just give me the goods."

I sigh, knowing this will go on until I do. "Yeah, the earth moved, okay?"

She squeals. "Awesome." She shakes my shoulder excitedly and I try not to groan at her enthusiasm. "So?"

"So what? That's all you're getting."

She scoffs. "Yeah, sure it is." Michael returns and she mutters before he sits down. "I'll beat it out of you later."

"Well he made the reservation about a month ago, so I think this was purely coincidental."

I'm relieved to say the least. "Thank you."

"So he isn't stalking you, which is good. But he's a little on the possessive side. Are we okay with this?" Michael asks hesitantly.

"I think if you two were holding hands, it was fair for him to be a bit alpha about it," Louise points out, turning to me. "Why were you two holding hands exactly?"

"That might be kinda your fault," I tell her.

"My fault? I wasn't even here."

"Michael had a really shitty day at work and I was telling him it was going to be okay."

"And that was my fault because...?"

"Because Michael works with Cami, remember?"

"Ohhhhhhhhhh," she says, realization dawning.

"Yeah, oh," Michael deadpans. "Cami on her best day is almost more than I can take, but Cami post breakup is like Carrie, having a really bad day."

"Shit," Louise says under her breath.

"Let's just say that I spent most of the day trying to convince a high-profile Hollywood client that 'How about I shove my boot in your ass', means something totally different in the UK than it does in the US. Now I have to take the client on myself, or we lose him."

"Sheesh. Sorry, I guess." She sighs. "It was unavoidable."

"What happened?"

Our drinks arrive and she takes a huge gulp of hers before she tells us anything.

"You've met Cami, right?" she says flatly.

"Yep," Michael and I say in unenthusiastic unison.

"Well then, do I really have to explain?"

I laugh, clapping my hand over my mouth. "I'm sorry."

"Nah, don't be. She's hard fucking work, dirty as all hell and an absolute firecracker in bed. But hard fucking work."

Michael winces and puts his hands over his ears. "No thank you. Nope. Don't need to hear that."

Louise laughs and rolls her eyes. "It had to come to an end eventually. There's only so much a phenomenal tongue can make up for."

"Oh for the love of—" Michael shakes his head vigorously from side to side, perhaps trying to shake the mental images out.

"So you're okay about it? You seem a little bummed, but it sounds like you've made peace with it."

"I have, but I'll still miss the orgasms."

I laugh. "Oh Louise."

Connor appears at the table looking hot and bothered. "So what can I get you?"

"Umm...a menu?" Louise replies, sounding exceptionally snarky. I don't know what's happened to her manners tonight, or why poor Connor is getting all her wrath.

"Oh I'm sorry," Connor says, with an equal measure of snark, turning to reach for one at a nearby station. He hands it to her with a flourish and then looks to Michael and I, glancing back at Louise briefly with a look of distain before addressing us with much more warmth. "And for the lady? I take it you'll be demolishing the usual?"

"I sure will. I'll even share it with these two."

Louise looks up from her menu. "What's the usual?"

"It's enough to feed a hungry bear," I tell her, whipping the menu out of her hands and handing it back to Connor. "She'll be having the usual too."

Connor takes the menu back, scribbling on another pad he pulled from his apron. "Very good." He bows to Louise, heaping on the sarcasm and I love him for it. "Anything else, ma'am?"

She downs the remainder of her two gulp martini and hands him the glass, retrieving the olives as an afterthought and pulling them off the stick with her teeth. "Another drink would be fantastic," she says around the olives.

"Sure thing." He takes the glass. "One martini, extra dirty." He smiles with false sincerity and turns away. "Hold the arsenic for now," he mutters.

Louise narrows her eyes at the back of him and I smirk and exchange a look with Michael.

Out of habit I take my phone out of my bag and look to see if I have any messages, even though the only two people who usually text me are right here. To my surprise there is a text though. From Rhys.

**Rhys:** All I can think about with you sitting over there is how good it feels to be in you.

I squeeze my knees together.

"Why are you grinning like a fool at your phone?" Louise asks.

"Umm. No reason." I look up guilty as hell.

"He's texting her. I can see him on his phone." Michael laughs.

Sure enough, another message pops up on my screen.

**Rhys:** I want to taste you again.

I feel the flutter in my belly and a flush prickles my skin.

"Jesus, you're blushing." Louise shakes her head in wonderment.

"Isn't he in a meeting?" I ask Michael, flatly refusing to give Rhys the satisfaction of turning around.

"His companion must be in the bathroom. He's alone right now," Michael confirms.

**Me:** You're in a meeting aren't you?

**Rhys:** I'm over it already. I'd rather be with you.

I will not turn around. I don't want him to know how much he affects me. I stare at my phone not knowing how to reply.

"I think we've lost her," Louise tell Michael. I look up guiltily.

"I'm sorry." I shove my phone back in my bag. "I can catch up with him later."

"That might be sooner than you think," Michael informs me. "His friend is back and it looks like they're wrapping things up." I watch as Michael not so subtly studies them and then he looks at me suddenly. "Oh shit. He's coming over."

We look up collectively when Rhys gets to our booth. He smiles and looks to my friends, rather than to me. "My meeting resolved itself rather quicker than I anticipated and I don't fancy eating alone. I was wondering if you would have room for one more?"

"Of course," Michael says right away. "Please have a seat." He indicates the space beside him and Rhys takes it gladly.

I feel weird pinned in by Louise while Rhys sits across the other side. I feel oddly protective toward him and I can't reach him from here. I wish he was beside me, but I can be an adult and sit through a meal with him just out of reach. I think.

"So, Rhys. Tell us about how you two got together. Charlotte here is giving us nothing."

Rhys laughs heartily. "A gentleman doesn't kiss and tell I'm afraid."

"Well shit," she huffs.

I smirk at her, then look at Rhys to find his eyes glittering and a knowing smile on his lips. He's thinking about last night. I can just tell.

"Oh God, she's blushing again."

I nudge Louise. "I am not."

After that, conversation turns to less personal things. The food, the hit the restaurant is right now, nothing deep. We don't talk about work or our home lives. It's light fun. Probably the most fun I've had in years. Rhys has hardly taken his eyes off me. I wish I could reach out to him or touch him under the table.

When the check comes, Rhys insists on picking it up. "No, honestly, I crashed your night, it's the least I can do." The look of confusion on his face when Michael's double comes over to take payment is so funny, we all laugh too hard to fight him on it.

I have to stifle a yawn. I barely slept last night after all.

"Tired, kitten?" Rhys asks softly.

Louise's eyebrows rise up into her hair on hearing the nickname.

I nod, trying to ignore the reaction.

"I can take you home if you like."

"No need," Louise says firmly, looking to me pointedly, telling me with her eyes to just go with it. "I'm coming back to your new place like we planned, right?"

I frown. "Oh, uh—yeah."

She nods encouragingly, once I follow her lead. I'm just not sure what I'm going along with exactly. I don't know why, but I guess she just settled where Rhys is going after we leave here and that would be not home with me.

"I can see you ladies back anyway, I get off on the same tube stop," he offers, seeming unaffected by the exclusion.

I look to Michael, feeling like we are leaving him out.

"I have to help Connor close tonight. One of his closers went home sick. It's the price I have to pay to have this kickass table at my beck and call. So if Rhys doesn't mind seeing you home I won't have to worry."

"It will be my pleasure," Rhys assures him.

We all stand to leave and Rhys shakes Michael's hand again. "It was nice meeting you, maybe we can all get together again?"

"Sounds good to me," Michael agrees. "I had fun tonight."

Rhys puts his hand on the small of my back as we walk outside. I shiver slightly.

"Would you like my coat?" Rhys whispers in my ear.

"No, I'm not cold, but thank you."

He gives me a knowing smirk. He knows exactly what he does to me.

We make our way to the tube station and ten minutes later we arrive at our stop. Rhys hasn't stopped touching me, a graze here, a light kiss there. We walk silently up toward the building and I pause. I'm about ready to get Louise an Uber back to her place.

"This is where I say good night." Rhys inclines his head then takes a step closer to give me a chaste kiss.

My fingers automatically go to my lips where they burn from his touch.

"Thank you for letting me intrude on your night, kitten." He takes a step away, I think needing the distance as much as I do.

"Great to meet you, Louise. I'll see you ladies later." Those damn butterflies are back.

Louise nudges me with her elbow. "Come on. Let's get inside." She throws an arm around my shoulder and turns me toward the door. "I can't wait to hear all the dirty details," she adds, low enough for only me to hear.

"Oh give it up," I groan.

"No, you'll be giving it up, not me. I want to know everything."

"Is that why you insisted on coming back here?"

"No, Char. That was because of that overwhelmed deer in headlights look you keep getting while he's undressing you with his eyes. I think what you need is a night sans dick, to decompress and think straight, or he's going to chew you up and spit you out."

"You don't think he's right for me?"

"I think he's perfect for you. I just want you to be the dynamite I know you are, not this—" She waves her hand gesturing to the whole of me. "Whatever is happening right now."

Louise chuckles and locks her arm tighter around me, walking me into the building. I really want to look over my shoulder to see if he is watching us go in.

"Don't do it," she whispers.

"Do what?" I hiss back.

"Look to see if lover-boy is watching."

"I really hate it when you do that." I press the button for the elevator up.

"I know." She giggles.

"Thank you."

"For what?"

"For knowing what I need."

"That's what best friends are for." She grins. "That and reliving every mind-blowing second of your new and amazing sex life."

"Oh Lord."

The elevator dings and we both step into it. I look up just as the doors are closing and Rhys blows me a kiss and winks. God damn he's sexy.

# SIXTEEN

The past week has dragged. I haven't seen Rhys since the elevator doors closed on him blowing me that kiss. Some family thing came up and he had to leave town and go back home to Scotland for a few days. He was apologetic, but with things moving so fast, I thought it would do us good to have some time to think.

I was grateful to Louise for forcing me to take a breath that night. If she hadn't invited herself home with me I would have spent another night tangled in Rhys, and as fantastic as that sounds, I think I would have gotten lost in him to the point where his absence for a whole week would probably leave me insane with self-doubt. Instead, I sat up half the night with my best friend, doing the very thing we were most looking forward to about me moving here and hadn't yet had the chance to do. Talking.

She made me tell her everything. Ev-er-y-thing! I was already in a dead relationship when she and I first met and in the years since, my sex life went from hardly worth a mention to tumbleweed territory. I've never had anything like this to discuss with her. I've never needed her advice or reassurance on whether I did or said the right thing, because there was nothing to talk about.

I had thought that I wouldn't like to share intimate details, because they are just that, intimate. But Louise has this way of pulling them out of you and before I knew what I was doing, I was giving her the play-by-play and hanging on her every word as she coached me through this dating thing.

Face to face girl time is something I have never had. I needed it. It helped put a few things in perspective for me. A relationship with Rhys is nothing more or less than two people seeing if they can give it a go. I shouldn't hold myself back because I might have regrets and I can't view it as a life changing and permanent decision because nothing is ever permanent. Louise told me to stop overthinking and second guessing and just let it happen.

I was disappointed when the next day I got a text from him telling me he was at the airport and would be away a few days, since I was ready to try out my new philosophy on life and love. But what I will say for a week of distance is that it has given me a good chance to get to know him better. Our nightly calls and regular texts have given us the space to learn a lot about each other without sex getting in the way.

He absolutely adores his mother and he's close with his brothers. I haven't asked about what exactly happened to his father, I only know he's gone and that he died suddenly. I'm sure he will tell me in his own time if he wants to. It obviously hurts him to talk about.

My phone goes off and I glance down and see it's a message from him.

**Rhys:** I miss you, kitten.

The message is accompanied by a photo and I swear my heart drops right into my panties. It's a rugged selfie of Rhys in the mountains. He's surrounded by the blooms of wild heather. It's simply breathtaking. *He* is simply breathtaking.

I stare at the phone and feel myself resisting telling him I miss him too. Has it been long enough to miss him? Then I think of Louise's advice. I can't hold myself back because I'll have regrets. If I miss him too then I should just say so. Still, I don't mind making him work for it a little, I smirk.

**Me:** Fishing for compliments?

**Rhys:** Maybe...

**Me:** It looks beautiful there.

**Rhys:** Come with me some time, I think you'd love it.

My stomach flutters at the promise of future trips and I ignore it.

**Me:** I would. The scenery looks amazing.

**Rhys:** Just the scenery?

**Me:** You ARE fishing for compliments.

**Rhys:** Just tell me you miss me too.

**Me:** Don't you think it's too soon for all of that?

**Rhys:** Not if it's true.

I touch my finger to the screen and trace his smile. I do miss him. Will I sound weak if I admit that to him? I swallow hard.

**Me:** I miss you too.

There's a knock on my office door and I jump, feeling guilty for daydreaming on the job. I toss my phone in my top drawer. "Come in," I call out, checking my calendar to make sure I don't have a meeting I forgot about. The door doesn't open and I frown.

Another knock sounds and I clear my throat to make sure I'm heard this time. "Come. In," I enunciate clearly.

Still nothing. I groan, getting up from my desk and walking to the office door. "Yes?" I bark as I pull open the door to reveal Rhys waiting expectantly, twirling a piece of heather between his fingers. My eyes go wide.

"I knew you missed me," he beams, stepping into the room and closing the door behind him.

Momentarily stunned into silence, I stare at him. The suit is back. He looks so self-assured standing there. So damn sexy. He holds out the heather to me and at once my thoughts of schooling my reception are gone and I throw myself into his arms. "Why didn't you tell me you were coming back?"

He wraps his arms tightly around me and I let his warmth sink in. "I wanted to surprise you." He leans back just slightly to look down at me, his intense gaze eating me up. He moves in until his lips brush softly over mine and whispers softly, "I've missed you more than I should." And then he kisses me.

I hum to life and groan with need as he wraps an arm around my waist, bringing me closer to him. I can feel the length of him pressed up against me. He moves me backwards into the room, the backs of my legs bumping into the edge of the desk. Without breaking the kiss he lifts me, sitting me on the desk. He breaks the kiss off, panting. "Next time I'm taking you with me."

"This is so crazy," I say in between my gasps.

"I know, I love it." He leans over me, his hand on the small of my back, and lays me down on the desk. Thankfully it was cleared, because I would have gladly thrown it all to the floor. I try to raise up but he holds me down, deepening the kiss and stepping between my legs.

My skirt rises up my thighs. I reach between us and unbuckle his belt, making quick work of freeing him.

He sucks in a sharp breath as my hand wraps around him. "I wanted to talk," he gasps. "Take things slow." His words say the opposite of what his body is telling me. "But it's going to have to wait, I need to be inside you. Now."

"Take me."

"I plan on it."

He pops the first, then second and third buttons of my blouse, skimming his fingers over the lace of my bra and studying it hungrily. "Mmmm too pretty to be hidden behind clothes," he murmurs, then dips his fingers inside one of the cups, pulling it down, exposing me to him. The second the cool air hits my sensitive nipple, I arch. He dips his head further and takes it into his mouth, then presses it between his teeth making me groan in pleasure.

"I need you," I plead, not caring where we are or what could happen. My hands are pulling at his clothes trying to get us skin to skin. He takes them into one of his and pulls them up over my head.

"You had control the first time, kitten, now it's time for you to see how I like to have control of everything, your need, your pleasure, your release. I want all of it to happen because of me. I want to give it all to you."

Something deep inside me melts. "I want to take it."

Rhys makes an approving sound and with one hand still holding my wrists back, he trails the other down my front. I hook a leg around his hips, my skirt hiking up completely around my waist.

"I'd love to have you naked in my bed, but I can't wait that long to have you. I have an urgent need for you, kitten." He reaches between my legs, pressing on my clit through my lace panties.

I whimper. "Please."

"Hold on to the edge of the desk," he demands, his voice husky and strained.

The moment my fingers grasp the edge of the desk, he releases my wrists and begins to worship my body with both hands, making me arch up off the desk. He pulls my panties off to one side, the cool air there doing nothing for the heat inside me.

"Please, Rhys."

"I'm going to take you so fiercely that I'll have to swallow your screams," he warns, placing himself right at my entrance. Then he leans over me and in one solid thrust, fills me completely. My mouth opens to express the ecstasy and he's there, devouring my cries. His tongue matches the rhythm of his hips. I let go of the desk and rake my nails down his back, he grunts and breaks the kiss.

"That's my kitten," he growls between thrusts.

I bring him in deeper with my heels. He leans down on the desk and braced by his forearms he peppers my face with kisses as he pumps into me.

"More," I moan. "I need more."

"It'll come, kitten." His pace feels so good it hurts, but I'm desperate to reach my peak. I try to slip a hand between us for a quicker release, but he takes mine into his and raises them above my head again, holding them there as he gains momentum. "I told you to hold on," he growls.

I don't know where I end and he begins, what I do know is how fantastic it feels. I stiffen as I feel the waves of pleasure cresting. My mouth opens to scream and I only get a gasp out as he takes my mouth again in a punishing kiss. He swallows my screams and groans into my mouth as he finds his own release.

We lay against my desk panting for a few moments, as we both try to catch our breath. Then when he finds the strength, he lifts up on his elbows and looks down at me.

"You're incredible."

"You're not so bad yourself." I smile, then turning more serious, I add something I want him to know. "And I really did miss you."

I hear something move outside my office door, the sound is nothing unusual, but it brings reality crashing down around us. My eyes go wide as I remember that we are in my place of work and my assistant has permission to come in whenever she needs me.

"We'll have to continue this later," Rhys says, recognizing the panic in me. He kisses me, then winces as he pulls out.

I quickly feel the loss of him as he lifts up, replacing my panties and tucking himself back into his pants. I sit up quickly buttoning my blouse. Once I've put myself back together I straighten everything out and pat my hair.

"You look fine." He chuckles.

"I'm sure I'm a mess."

"No, you suit the just fucked look. It's hot."

I smack his chest playfully. "If I have to look a mess, at least I rock it, is that what you're saying?"

"Basically."

Voices can be heard beyond my door, reminding us that this isn't the time or place. "I have work I need to do," I tell him, regretfully.

"I'll let you get back to it," he concedes. "I want to see you tonight. I'll come to your place, we can eat out or I can cook for you."

"Okay," I agree without hesitation.

"I need to spend some time *with* you, kitten, not just inside you. There are some things I want to tell you and they won't wait."

I nod, concerned by the ominous sound of his request. He doesn't seem concerned though, just sincere, and that takes some of the worry away.

He steps forward kissing me softly, it's only fleeting, but I find I can't let him go. Dragging him against me by his lapels, I deepen the kiss, wishing he didn't have to leave. After extracting himself, fixing his tie and pecking me once more on the lips, he slips silently out the door without another word.

I feel spent and wobbly when I walk back to my desk. It's then that I realize it's past lunchtime and I haven't eaten anything today. I collect my purse and head out of my office, not knowing where I will go for food, but knowing if I don't I'll end up with a headache and be no good when Rhys comes over.

"Oh hey, Charlotte. Are you okay?" John asks when I almost run into him in the hall. "You look a little peaked."

"Yeah, I just missed lunch. I'm going to run out and grab something before I run out of steam." I feel a blush creep up my face when I think about exactly how I just spent the last of my energy.

"Yes, you do that. We need you sharp," he chuckles. "You have to take care of yourself."

"I will." I smile and head for the elevators. As I press the call button, I run over my food options. Fast and close are best, but I can't think of a thing I want, when suddenly I remember the box of BBQ leftovers I took home last night, which are still sitting in my fridge. When the elevator arrives I select my apartment floor rather than the lobby and my stomach growls in anticipation.

My upward dash to my late lunch is thwarted briefly when the elevator stops on the eleventh floor. I step aside to let three people in and the doors begin to close. That's when I see something that has me shooting my hand out to halt the door.

Level ten is the wellness center. A place I have yet to visit. But I find myself walking slowly out of the elevator, toward the reception area, confused and lacking any words.

Seersha, or something, John had called it. So why am I looking at another word? One I have seen before, tattooed across the chest of the man who has just had his way with me in my office.

SAORSA WELLNESS CENTRE is painted in soft hues behind the welcome desk. I stare, not knowing what to make of the coincidence. It has to be a coincidence, right?

Interrupting my thoughts, a young woman stands to greet me. "Welcome to Seersha, how may I help you?"

I barely take my eyes off the word behind here when I ask, "Seersha?"

She smiles like she gets this question all the time. She follows my stare to the logo and points. "It's pronounced seer-sha, it' Gaelic I believe. It means freedom. Are you new to the company?"

"Hmm?" I murmur, mulling over her words, then tear my eyes away and focus on her. "Yes, I started a few weeks ago."

She smiles warmly. "Would you like a tour?"

"I—" I glance at my wrist. No watch. "I can't, I have a meeting soon. Maybe I could come back another time?" I start to back away, all of a sudden feeling an urgency to get away. Question after question is forming and I might burst if I don't leave right now.

"Of course, you are welcome any time. Let me give you our brochure and workshop timetable to look at at your leisure and when you have time you can pop back for a guided tour of our facilities."

I nod, taking the booklet she hands me, looking again at the word on the wall and feeling the pressure of unanswered questions build. Turning back to the elevators, I triple press the call button impatiently. It comes up three floors and is mercifully empty when I step in. Food forgotten, I press my office floor. The ride down is painfully slow. I stare blankly at the brochure in my hand, not letting any of my questions really gain any traction. When my eyes focus on the cover, I see that word again and beneath it a definition:

*Freedom, Salvation, Redemption, Liberty.*

Rhys' explanation echoes in my mind as I read the words.

This can't be a coincidence. The elevator arrives on my floor and I hurry back to my office, closing the door behind me. I toss my purse and the brochure on my desk and sit heavily in my chair. I turn to my computer and bring up Google. My mind is in full scale riot mode by now. I have so many theories and questions it's hard to know where to start, but one thought keeps pushing its way to the forefront and my fingers start typing.

Rhys... I hover over the keys, not knowing if I want to know what I'm about to discover. But I have to find out. I rush to type the second word before I change my mind... McAllister.

# SEVENTEEN

I don't know why it surprises me at this point, but when Rhys' face fills the screen again and again, I sit back, astonished.

How? More importantly, why? I cringe as I scroll and find several of them are of him with Lisa. Gag. Knowing better, but not being able to stop myself, I click on one and the article that opens up about some charity event quotes them as Entrepreneur Rhys McAllister and companion Elisabeth King. I grab the file I left on my desk and turn to the first page. ELISKIN. Of course.

I close my eyes and sigh.

It's not the fact that he's my boss. Granted I would hesitate to get involved with someone at work because, been there-done that, but that's not why I feel so betrayed. It's the fact that he lied to me this whole time. I snatch my phone from my bag and scroll to his name in my contacts. What the hell am I going to say? Growling in frustration, I drop it onto the desk. Then having second thoughts I pick it up again.

**Me:** I need you.

I hit send and wait for the reply, it doesn't take long. It never does when I text those words.

**Louise:** What's up?

**Me:** Not much, just found out I'm screwing my boss is all.

**Louise:** STFU!!!

**Me:** He doesn't know I know. I don't know what to do.

**Louise:** Talk to him?

Fucking Louise, always so cool, calm and collected. Just once I'd like to see her freak the fuck out. She makes it sounds so easy. "Just talk to him," I mumble to myself.

**Me:** I'm freaking out. He lied to me!

**Louise:** He told you he wasn't the owner?

*"Damn her!"* I hiss in my empty office.

**Me:** No, he didn't tell me he wasn't the owner.

**Louise:** Did you ask?

**Me**: That's not the point and you know it!

**Louise:** You need to calm down, Char.

Wrong thing to say to someone freaking out, Louise.

**Me:** I'm pissed.

We are so used to talking through text that I'm sure it doesn't even cross her mind to call. Or she knows I won't pick up the phone. I want to scream, but instead I get up and pace back and forth trying to spend the excess energy another way while I think about what I'm going to do.

I'm fucking the boss.

I feel sick. Everything I tried to escape and change about my life, I'm doing all over again.

**Louise:** Talk to him, I'm sure there is a reason he didn't tell you.

**Me:** Oh… I'm going to talk to him alright. I'll text you later.

**Louise:** Charlotte…

I ignore the message and continue to pace.

How do I even approach him?

My relentless phone starts buzzing with a call and I look

down, seeing a picture of Louise and I on the screen. Well what do you know, she's game for rejection obviously. I hit ignore. I know she'll be all logical and use reason and all that jazz but, I. Am. Pissed. Besides, I'll only snap at her and none of this is her doing.

Christ, what the hell am I going to do?

My phone buzzes again, with a text this time.

**Louise:** Want me to come over?

**Me:** No.

**Louise:** I will be there in thirty minutes.

**Me:** Don't. I mean it, Louise. I'll figure this out.

Then I pause to remind myself I'm not being kind. I text her, not the other way around.

**Me:** I'm sorry. I'll be okay, I promise.

**Louise:** OK. Just talk to him. He might have a good explanation.

I scoff into my empty office. How can I be so invested in such a short time? I can see where I went wrong every step of the way. I never asked where he worked, or even what his last name was. That would have solved all the problems right there. I would have gotten there eventually, but I was so swept up in the thrill of him, how he consumed me and bent me to his will. My whole life until this point I have been in control. Henry wasn't the alpha type, he let me run everything. I controlled everything. The house, the business, even when and how and more importantly, *if* we would have sex. I controlled it all. I didn't set out to, but someone had to lead and it turned out to always be me.

That was part of our problem. I see that now.

The way I see it, I have a clear choice to make. I can rip him a new ass over text and pack it all up. Quit and go back to Louise's house, never to see him again. That's the kind of route I would have taken in my old life. The 'why deal with shit when you can just distance yourself?' approach. OR... I can face it, see what he has to say. Actually hear him out. I don't think there can be a good excuse, but part of me really wants one. Don't I at least deserve a face to face explanation? Deep down in my heart I know the decision is made. And however weak it makes me feel, I want him to have a good excuse, because I really freaking like him.

I've achieved so much in my life and I always meet challenges head on, but when it comes to emotions, I've run from everything difficult to face. When I caught Henry cheating I didn't even try and fight for us, I left. I placed the blame solely on him, even though I know deep down I was a part of the problem.

My pacing is halted by a light tap on my office door. I look up to see the handle turn and John appears, frowning, in the doorway.

"Everything okay, John?"

"Not really, Marie had a fall, they've taken her to hospital. She may have broken something."

"Oh no, John. That's terrible."

He frowns and I see the worry etched into the lines. "I'm heading home to be with her. I might need to take a couple of days. I'll call in and let you know more tomorrow and work from home until I know what's going to happen."

"Don't worry about a thing here. Is there anything I can do?"

"No, it's fine. I'm just going to run these up to Mr. McAllister and then I'll be off. I have a car coming, so I won't stop. I just wanted to let you know." He lifts the folder in his hand and taps it.

"I'll take them," I blurt. I don't know what possessed me but I'd like to help John out and it will give me the opportunity I need not to run, but to turn and face this like it needs to be faced.

As I think about it, I know this couldn't be more perfect.

John hesitates. "Are you sure? I mean, he's not in his office, he's at home, in the penthouse."

"Of course," I assure him with more confidence than I feel. "I can drop it off for you, it won't take a minute and our first meeting is long overdue anyways. You get home to your wife and don't worry about a thing."

"If you don't mind, that would be great. Thank you." He hands me the folder and goes to turn away. "Oh wait, you'll need this." He reaches into his inside pocket and produces the keycard required to make the elevator go to the top floor. "Thanks again, Charlotte."

"No worries, I hope it's nothing serious, but seriously, take whatever time you need. Everything will still be here when you get back."

I say this with the knowledge that I might not be. But he doesn't need that stress right now.

John heads back to his office to gather his things and I walk slowly to the elevator and press the button. My mind is going a hundred miles a minute with things I want to say, but still I have no words. No way of knowing how this is going to go down. I can't even put an opening line together in preparation. I have to take deep calming breaths. I step in and insert the card, then press the button for the penthouse. My heart is hammering, threatening to burst out of my chest as the elevator rises. When it stops, the doors slide open to reveal a small foyer. I step out and stare at the door on the other side, imagining Rhys on the other side of it. Suddenly, it's too much and I turn to run, but the doors close and the elevator descends, leaving me stranded, with no choice but to face my problems.

"You can do this, Charlotte," I say to the empty hallway.

I step up to the door. I can't hear anything but the pounding of my heart. I press a shaky finger into the doorbell and take a small step back. I'm sure there has to be a security system up here. I wonder if he will open the door if he sees it's me?

I hear the soft padding of feet and hold my breath. No turning back now.

The door opens and Rhys, with a towel slung low on his hips and another covering his head as he rubs vigorously, drying his hair, stands aside expectantly to let me pass.

My mouth goes dry. His beautifully inked chest and arms flex as he dries himself off.

"Come on in, John," he says, turning back into the room.

"Mr. McAllister," I hiss with a quiver in my voice.

The towel drops out of his hand and he turns, his wild hair falling in his face and his eyes wide with shock. We both just stare at each other in silence, for what feels like forever. Then finally, he blinks.

"Kitten?" he whispers.

# EIGHTEEN

I can't do this. I won't give him the opportunity to lie to me. I turn back toward the elevator.

"No, wait!" he pleads. "Please don't go."

I hear his footsteps coming closer to me and swallow hard. I reach out to press the elevator button and his voice follows me out.

"Kitten, just let me explain."

Breathe, Charlotte. Breathe. I turn back toward him and my heart stills as I see his face. I march up to him and push the file into his chest.

"Here is the new policy I wrote, to prevent what happened with *Lisa,* from ever happening again." I emphasize her name so that he knows damn well I've put the whole thing together.

He catches it against his chest and lets out a breath, causing his shoulders to slump.

I suck in my lower lip, biting it to keep me from saying anything I'll regret.

"Will you come in?"

I shake my head. I regret coming up here. I just want to leave.

But I know I need the answers to all of my questions or eventually they will eat me alive.

"Please, Charlotte, I owe you an explanation. Just hear me out and then if you still want to leave, I won't stop you."

I don't respond, but I don't leave either. Rhys takes this as a sign that I plan to stay and gestures toward his open door, encouraging me forward. Reluctantly, I place one foot in front of the other and he steps aside allowing me to enter his penthouse. Stopping just past the door I wait for him to close it.

"Come in, sit. Let me throw on some trackies quickly and then we can talk."

I nod and follow him deeper into his home.

"I'll be right back." He places the folder down on the table in the entryway and turns toward a hallway, then he pauses. "You won't leave, will you?"

I shake my head, not trusting my voice, or even knowing if I can promise I won't run the moment he's out of sight.

"Okay." He nods and darts into a room off the hall.

The moment he's gone, I feel the itch to leave.

I can't bear for him to lie to me and worse, to fall for it. The only way to protect myself from that is not to even hear him out. To withdraw and stay in control of my own fate.

Fuck this.

I'm about to make for the door when I glance around the room. Something stops me. More than that, something draws me in. Walking on unsteady legs through the foyer I venture further into his world. I take in my surroundings and wonder, who is this man?

When you say the word penthouse, you picture something stark and cold. A space purely for show. A penthouse is usually a status symbol, not a home. Not this place, though. This place is lived in. Warm and cozy. I feel like I've just stepped into a highlands hunting lodge, not that I've ever been in one of those, but the room has that kind of feel. The den is all warm tones and rich plaids. Old leather and soft pillows, seasoned wood and heritage. There's no other word for it.

Dozens of photographs line the walls, and even knowing that I'm being drawn in beyond the point of escape, I can't help but get closer to them for a glimpse of the life he lives. So far I've only been offered lies and omissions. These photos are his truth and I need to see them.

There's one of Rhys with a bunch of men on a mountainside. An old wedding photo of a young couple I would assume are his parents. Rhys looks a lot like his dad if that's him. In the center, one is bigger than the rest and it's of an older woman, surrounded by five young men, one of whom is Rhys. The men must be his brothers, because they are all looking inwards at their mother with such adoration, while she beams at the lens.

This is not the home of someone who has no regard for people's feelings. The man who lives here is sentimental and family oriented.

Rhys comes back into the living area, shirtless and out of breath. "You're still here," he whispers in relief.

"Surprised?"

He nods and runs his fingers through his damp hair. "Very."

"Well today is just full of surprises." I can't fight the hint of bitterness in my words and I can tell they cut through him by the look on his face.

"I thought for sure when I finally told you, you'd be done with me. That's why it has taken me so long."

"Don't you think I deserved the truth? Instead I had to find out for myself," I snap.

He hangs his head. "I know. I'm sorry."

"Do you know how humiliating it's going to be to have to leave my job because I fucked the boss?"

His eyes fly up to mine. "Leave? But— you can't leave.

Liberty needs you." Deep lines cut into his forehead. He reaches out a hand to test the water, but I pull out of his reach, instead turning to look at the pictures again for some distance.

"I don't want you to leave Liberty. I'll step back if I have to. Please just agree to stay."

All the small details of what he's asking of me run through my head. The thought of facing the people I work with once they know I've been fraternizing. John...God I can't. The embarrassment of them knowing that I not only replaced Lisa in the company, but also in the boss' bed. It's so nasty. What if they think that's how I got the job? What if?—

I lose myself in the what ifs and I only realize I've been silent for a while when Rhys breaks into my thoughts.

"That's my mum," he says fondly of the woman in the family portrait I was studying earlier. As I suspected. "She thinks you should go with me next time I visit. She says I'd better not fuck it up before she gets to meet you."

I turn to face him, surprised by his nearness. "You told your mom about me?"

"Of course. Why does that surprise you?"

"Um, I don't know? Maybe because you didn't tell me a whole bunch of stuff you should have, so I guess I'm shocked to know you told your mom of all people."

He steps closer. "Kitten, I know I should have—"

I hold up my hand, stopping him from getting too close. I don't trust myself with him close to me. "Don't," I say firmly.

"My mum warned me this would happen. She said I needed to stop delaying the inevitable and tell you everything."

"But instead you chose to ignore her and let me find out for myself?"

"No. I planned to tell you today. As soon as I got back."

"So why didn't you?"

Rhys looks away not able to meet my eyes.

I fold my arms across my chest waiting him out. Why should I make this easy on him?

"Because," he sighs. "You looked so incredible when I saw you today. I needed to have you. I couldn't wait. And if that was going to be our last time together, I couldn't let it pass. I had to make it count."

"Was it worth it?"

He reaches out again and this time, I don't prevent him making contact. He strokes his fingers down my arm, but doesn't attempt to deepen the connection. "Being with you will always be worth it. But if the price is losing you for good, then it's too high."

"How long, Rhys?"

"How long what?"

I raise my eyebrows, waiting, knowing he knows what I mean.

"How long have I known you were working for me?"

I nod, trying to remain firm, all the while wrapping my arms across my chest in an attempt to protect myself from the answer coming.

Rhys sighs. "I didn't know when I met you in the airport. Or in the club that first night." He runs his fingers through the damp strands, arranging them with effortless perfection. "I found out when I was putting together your welcome pack and saw the photo of you HR had put on your security pass."

I watch as he relives the memory and am struck by the pained expression his face holds. "It is like a punch in the gut. Here I was, confident I was hiring someone we couldn't live without, then I come to discover it's someone I—" He cuts himself off and looks away.

"Someone you what, Rhys?" I demand, lacking patience.

Rhys turns back searching my eye, looking so unsure. "Someone I can't live without," he whispers.

I choke. "Wha—? But— You barely knew me then! We'd spoken twice."

"That doesn't mean I didn't know, kitten. I knew when I saw you sitting down with your coffee and that pastry you destroyed that you were someone special. I just knew, okay? Don't tell me you didn't feel something similar, because I know you did. This thing between us hasn't gotten off to the best start and I take responsibility for that, but it was there from the moment we met and you know damn well it's true."

I open my mouth to disagree, but I can't. I press my lips together and remain silent, knowing in doing so that I'm effectively admitting as much, but to argue would be futile. I knew too. I didn't go looking for it. Hell, I couldn't even admit it to myself at first, but it was there all the same.

"Don't give up on me," he whispers.

I study him. The look of desperation he's wearing almost has me caving in. His bare chest and defined muscles and all that ink I didn't know I could love so much, offer a welcome distraction from the emotions he stirs in me, but then I realize I'm merely being sucked in another way. When my eyes fall on the word on his chest that was ultimately his undoing, I sigh in defeat. This is going to happen one way or another. I'm in too deep to just up and run, but I can't think with him half naked. "I'm willing to talk," I tell him. "But can you please put a shirt on?"

His lips part and a slow knowing grin appears on his face. "Of course. Now, that I know you aren't leaving, I'll get dressed properly. Just give me a quick second." He steps back, still holding my gaze and then turns and heads back down the hallway.

I move further into the room, running my hand over a tartan blanket that's folded over the back of the leather sofa. Everything about the room is comforting. I feel at ease enough to sit, despite the situation. I walk around the sofa and into the sitting area, deciding to sit where he can't sit too close. Sinking into the large armchair, I pull a pillow into my lap instinctively. As if a wad of stuffing in a plaid cover could offer me any sort of real protection. It's all I have to hold on to though, so I cling to it, cursing myself for the weakness.

Rhys reappears, this time wearing a hastily slung on shirt with his sweatpants, looking just as hurried as the last time. I take a small amount of satisfaction in the fact that he still wasn't completely convinced I'd stick around. It's mildly reassuring to think that he might be feeling as uncertain as I am.

Not hiding his relief, he comes around and sits gingerly right on the edge of the sofa, across from me.

"I really am sorry, if it means anything," he begins tentatively.

I slowly close my eyes to try and gather my control. "You should have said something."

He shakes his head. "No, I couldn't. Not when I found out."

"I think you're wrong."

"Hear me out." He cuts me off, his voice commanding my cooperation. "Let's be honest, kitten, you'd have run a mile. The person I was headhunting, I knew had just sold her company, to her ex-husband no less, for less than market value after a protracted and from all accounts bitter period of negotiation. You'd just made a fresh start, you weren't about to get tangled up with your new boss. And I knew we needed you here.

"I went after you for your work ethic and your success story. I had no idea about the woman behind the steely business decisions, award winning performance and game changing financial skills. I didn't know at the time how bad things were with Lisa, but I knew enough was enough. And with the plans we have for Liberty over the next few years, Lisa was going to be way out of her depth. I had to have you to help us get to where I know we are going to go. So hell no I couldn't risk you hating me and walking away."

"So that's all I am, an awesome CFO?"

"Shit, no! I'm mucking this all up." He stands and starts pacing. "You don't really think that do you?"

"No." I shrug. "But I wanted to hear you say it."

"That's evil, kitten."

"I think you can handle it, Rhys."

He drags his fingers through his hair and then comes to stand in front of me, bending to perch on the corner of the coffee table so that we are eye to eye. "I wouldn't be so sure about that. I'm fighting a losing battle here and you're toying with me." He shakes his head disapprovingly, but the corner of his mouth curls in a hint of a smile.

I try to ignore the softening of his features. I liked it better when he looked wracked with guilt and sick with worry. It's easier to stay firm when he's that way.

"You know you are more than that to me. From the moment I first saw you, you were more than that. And when I found out who you really were, I felt like I'd already lost you. I couldn't face meeting you on your first day, it was too raw. I didn't want to destroy your first day at your new job and selfishly I wanted to delay killing all possibility of getting to know you better for just a little while. I knew the truth would come out, I was just putting the moment off a little. Then we kept running into each other outside work and I couldn't fight the chances I was being given to steal time with you before it was over. Before I knew it, I was actively hiding from you at work to prolong my time with you." He bites at his bottom lip and looks away guiltily. "I know it was wrong, but every time I swore I would come clean, I would see you again and each time was better than the last. I knew how you would react and I just couldn't—"

"You don't know how I would have reacted. You never gave me the chance."

"Let me ask you this. Would you have gone out with me had I been there to welcome you to the company that morning and told you that I had only just found out myself, but I still wanted to see you?"

"No," I answer immediately.

"Exactly."

"But I still deserved to know."

"Maybe." He sighs. "But I felt like we both deserved to know what could happen between us, kitten. Are you sorry I gave us room to find out?"

I frown. "That isn't a fair question."

"Only because you don't want to have to admit the true answer," he counters softly, daring at last to reach out and touch me.

His fingers rest over my hand clasped tight around his pillow, but I don't acknowledge the move. Instead I close my eyes to gather my thoughts, he's right. I wouldn't have given him the time of day and yet I'm not sorry I got to see how things could be with him. I avoid giving him an answer by changing directions. "What I don't understand is, how did you know from the first time we met that you were so interested in me that you were willing to gamble my feelings?"

"I just did, kitten. I can't explain it. From the first time we talked, all I could think was, *she's the one.*"

The look on his face is so self-assured. He has absolute confidence in himself and how he feels. How am I such a fucking mess? "She's the one?" I raise a brow.

"God, I want to hold you." He sighs, then squares his shoulders resisting the need that might risk pushing me further away. I feel for him, but I'm still too rattled to take pity on him so I ignore his words.

"Yeah, the one," he continues. "Mum would always tell us growing up, you'll know when you meet the one and you'll do anything to keep them. It won't be in your control, you'll just be along for the ride."

I resist the urge to scoff. "Is that some type of crazy folklore your mom believes in?"

He blinks twice and then barks out the loudest laugh I've ever heard from him. "Mum is going to absolutely adore you."

I frown. "It was a serious question."

"I know and trust me, my brothers and I have been saying that for years. But she's not crazy. Whatever it is, it's real. I know that now because it's happened." He leans forward, gaining courage when I don't leap up to get away from him, and when he reaches out to stroke the backs of his knuckles down my face, I don't even flinch. "Give us a chance," he pleads softly. "Please."

I lean in to his touch before I can stop myself and then come to my senses. "It's not that simple, Rhys."

"Yes it is."

"No. It's not!" I growl. "You're still my boss." Then realization, no, obviously I'd already realized hits me. This is just actual acknowledgment of the awful facts, but they land heavily on my conscience all at once. "Oh God, I had sex with my boss on my desk." I hide my face in my hands.

I hear something unexpected. Rhys chuckles. "Not just sex, kitten. Great sex."

I look up at him and glare. "Really, Rhys? This is serious you know."

"I think you're overreacting just a wee bit."

Anger flashes through me and I cut him a look that has had lesser men cowering for mercy. "Personally, I think you are *under*-reacting just a 'wee bit'," I mimic his accent in my retort.

"I just know what I want and I'm not afraid to go after it."

I groan. "This is such a clusterfuck. It can't happen."

"Are you telling me we're done?"

"I don't know what else to say, Rhys."

The look of horror that crosses his face surprises me. "I'll pass all control to John, if I have to. Don't end what we have, Charlotte. Please."

"How can you say that? Don't you care about your company at all?"

"Of course I do, but it isn't important enough to stop me from living the life I want to live. Don't you see? Working isn't the same as living. Living is joy and sadness, fear and happiness. You can get those things from work, sure, but they don't keep you warm at night."

I watch him incredulously and blurt the first thought that comes into my head. "I don't understand how you're so sure of yourself while I am doubting every move I make."

Rhys sits back a little, giving me space to breathe, but he takes hold of my hand and keeps it between his as he begins to open up to me. "I used to be solely focused on making money. It's how I was raised. I came from money, but we were all taught that independence was everything. We have a strong family business, we could have all drifted into that and grown lazy, but Dad was adamant. Make it on your own first. There was no free ride in my family."

"That's commendable, I guess," I say, feeling that while the lesson was positive, there was something cold about it.

"Not really," Rhys laments. "My father taught all of us boys well when it came to business sense, but his unspoken rule was always money first, everything else second. There was no room for family on the top of his list of priorities. He missed every game, every concert, every sickness. He was proud of us, but the attachment was missing. All of our lives that's how we lived, that was our example. We don't talk about it, but it has affected us all in our own way. Hell, all of us are still unmarried.

"But mum...she'll do anything for those she loves and trust me she loves us enough for the both of them. She gave up her life to raise us and was just waiting on the day my father would retire and they would finally start the life she always dreamed about. Traveling the world and taking time to be with their family. Only that day never came. My father died alone in his office one night at work. We were all so used to him being at the office that we didn't notice he never came home. His personal assistant found him the next morning."

"Oh my God, Rhys," I gasp. "That's horrible."

"We all promised our mum after that fiasco that we would never put work first. It was an easy promise to make, but a hard one to keep. When you're young and growing successful, it's like a drug." He pauses and we exchange a look of knowing. We have both been in that place and I carry my own regrets from it. "I was so hungry. I let it consume me for a while." He looks pained and full of remorse. "But I woke up when I saw what it was doing to mum."

He swallows. "I took myself away from it all for a while. Travelled the far east, learned from the ways of life I was exposed to. It gave me a new perspective. I realized I'd gotten it all completely wrong. It was a liberation. It's crazy I know, but I had been so tightly wound, trying to establish myself as a man to be taken seriously, that I lost sight of who I was. Just like Dad had. In letting it all go I found not only myself, but also power. Not power over others like he always craved. Power over myself. And kitten, once you have that, you can't be anything but sure of yourself.

"Of course my company matters. I've worked damn hard to build it and I have plans to watch it grow. But it isn't all I have in my life. I would be content as an observer if that's what it takes to have you. What good is all the success and money I have if I have no one to share it with?"

"But you had Lisa," I spit, unable to stop myself. It's easier to cling on to the argument than admit his words have taken hold.

"I told you, we were never a couple and she knew that," he replies calmly.

"Are you sure? She seemed to think you were headed down the aisle if you ask me."

Rhys lets out a long sigh. "Her father had the idea in his head that she and I would end up married, but I never encouraged the notion. And Lisa...well who knows what's going on in her head half the time."

"You really let them think too much," I scold.

"It was convenient. I never lied, I was always upfront with her. She always gave me the impression it was mutual, so anything she created or expected outside of that is on her."

I huff. It's hard to be satisfied with the explanation when she's still the specter over whatever it is we have, but he's being honest, I know it. So I air another concern.

"Why didn't you press charges? Make me understand that."

He let out a breath. "My friendship with her father..."

"Rhys, that doesn't give her the right to steal millions from you."

"Let me finish. He was my father's best friend. After Dad died, he really stepped in. He helped me through the worst time in my life and gave me unlimited support. Emotional, practical, financial. He was more a father to us than Dad had ever known how to be and we all think a great deal of him. I, however, formed the closest bond with him. I would do anything to return the kindness he's shown me."

"Including turning a blind eye while his princess bleeds you dry?"

"Kitten," he warns. "I may have been naive as to the extent of her problem, but I was not turning a blind eye. I've done all I can to help her and I've supported him in every decision about her welfare, even those I disagreed with, because I owe him my unequivocal support."

"That still doesn't make it okay. What about everything you've lost?"

"Charlotte, he's paid me back all the money she stole."

I let my breath out with a whoosh. "Well, that would have been great information to have yesterday."

"I went back to Scotland so that we could discuss everything. Thanks to your skills we have a record of every penny. He begged me not to press charges. I wanted to you know, but I can't do that to him. Watching his daughter become what she is, is hard enough on the man. I won't be the reason he suffers more."

It's really difficult to be mad at him when he's being so considerate, so generous. "You're really not out any money?"

"No. And I'm done with Lisa for good. He loves her, but he knows she needs a lot of help and I think he finally realizes her future is not with me. I just didn't have a reason to cut the final tie until I met you."

"What makes me different?"

Rhys smiles. "I know what matters in life, and kitten, it's you."

I stare dumbfounded, unable to say anything in response to that declaration. All I can muster is an incoherent stammer. "Bu — I—" I pull my hand out of his and press it to my chest in the vain hope it will ease some of the pressure there.

He reaches forward patiently and takes it back in his, squeezing it reassuringly. "Kitten, you have to let go. You're letting control rule you."

Louise's words of wisdom echo in the silence that follows his statement. Am I so transparent that they could both reach the same conclusion about my core problem in just one conversation?

Apparently so.

And if they're right, what then?

"I don't know any other way, Rhys." Panic is rising in me to the point of breathlessness. "I've always been the boss," I pant.

"The person that ran things, the one people could count on. Who can I count on but myself?"

"Me," he whispers.

"I don't know how," I admit.

"Just let go. Just know that you aren't alone, I'm here. You don't need to control everything, some things can't be controlled. Like what you feel for me for example. You might think you can shut it off to protect yourself, but you can't. You can't control your natural feelings. You need to let some of them out if you want to enjoy life to the fullest."

I shake my head and pull my hand out of his, using it to hide my face from him. "You don't understand, Rhys. Whenever I care about someone or something I lose it. Both my parents, Henry and my company. If I don't keep these walls up then Lord knows what will happen in my life or how I'll be hurt."

"Kitten, baby, that's no way to live." He cups my face. "Structure, you live for it, but it isn't going to protect you forever. You don't need that wall, you need to tear it down." Leaning forward he presses his lips gently to mine. "I can help you."

I swallow past the lump in my throat. Suddenly I want to try. He makes me want more than I've had before. Do I dare to dream? "I— I need your help. Will you show me?"

His shoulder slump in relief. "Oh kitten, it's all I want." He stands and holds out a hand to me.

I know once I take that hand that my life won't be the same again. He makes me feel as though I could fly and I trust him to help me land safely. I settle my hand into his and stand.

# NINETEEN

"Take me to bed, Rhys."

He cocks his head and gives me a slow smirk. "Okay, let's start as we mean to go on. I will take you to bed, but let's be clear, it's only because I happen to agree with you that we are going to my bedroom. No more ordering me about, kitten."

I suppress a small smile. The first in hours. "Okaaay..." I answer hesitantly. Humor aside, his words awaken something in me. Something deep that I never knew existed. And when he takes a step toward his bedroom, I willingly follow behind him. It feels so natural to follow and with each step we take I am more sure of my decision.

His phone shatters the intense silence as we pass through the entrance and he stiffens, pausing.

"So close," I lament, chuckling as I lay my forehead on his shoulder in frustration.

"Ignore it," he groans, pulling me with more intent toward the bedrooms.

I stop him. "You may as well get it now. Last time it was Lisa having a meltdown and she wouldn't take the hint when you ignored it."

"It's not going to be Lisa," he assures me. "And honestly I don't care if it is. Ignore it. They will go away."

I tug him back. "Rhys, I'm not going anywhere okay? Just answer the phone first, then you can turn it off and relax."

He narrows his eyes at me. "Was that you ordering me around again by any chance?"

I press my lips together and fight a grin, shaking my head from side to side.

"Good." The ringing stops and Rhys looks triumphant. Then it begins again and I have to bite my lip to not say I told you so. "Motherfucker." He lets go of my hand and stalks over to the coffee table. snatching up his phone. "Yes?" he barks into the receiver, walking purposefully back over to me. Then he stops, frowning. "I told you not to let her in the building."

My stomach drops. I was joking when I brought her up, but I know beyond a doubt that the 'her' Rhys wants kept from the building has to be Lisa.

"Put her somewhere out of the way for God's sake and I'll be right down."

I become aware that I've taken a step back from him when he reaches out for me as he ends the call. He looks at me imploringly and I instinctively take another step back. "Lisa strikes again," I mutter.

"Kitten," he cautions, closing the space and taking my hand in his, even though I try to pull it out of his reach.

I close my eyes as he lifts it to his lips, trying to protect myself from the situation. Just when I think I can relax, she's back. "Go. You said you'd be right down." I can't keep the bitterness from my voice.

"I will be, but you're coming with me." He lays another kiss on my knuckles, clasping my hand in both of his.

I jerk back in shock. "I don't think that's a good idea, Rhys."

"It's the only way I'm going," he informs me.

I stare at him, he's the picture of calm and I have no idea how. I'm the opposite. "I—" I try to think of the words to convey what a supremely bad idea it would be for me to go see her with him. "I don't think she will like that."

It's feeble.

"I don't care what she would like. She had her final warning from me when she broke into the office."

I choke. "She—?"

Rhys nods in affirmation. "That night she broke down, it was at Liberty. She tried to gain access to the system after you cut off her active card we had missed."

I shake my head. "You said your place, I thought you meant home."

"Well they are one and the same really, aren't they? I guess I can admit that aloud now." He sighs. "She came in at night banking on the fact that the night guard probably didn't know she'd had her security clearance revoked. She told him she had left her pass in her office and he let her in. Needless to say I had every code and system changed that night to stop it from happening again and every member of security now knows she is not to be allowed in the building."

"And still, she's here."

"She's creating a scene in reception. Says she has something to tell me."

"I see," I snarl. "And you're going to go running down there and give her the satisfaction of knowing she still has you at her beck and call are you?"

Rhys shakes his head slowly. "Nope. I'm going to go down there and make sure that she never wants to come back." The tone he uses is so cold it startles me. I've never seen a side to him which gives me pause, but this Rhys...I don't think I'd cross him.

He looks thunderous for just a moment and then he blinks and it's gone.

"I want you with me. I think you need to hear what I have to say as much as she does. Come on." He pulls my hand and leads me along the hall. Bemused, I simply follow.

My first view of his bedroom takes my breath away, it's all natural wood with warm rugs and flannel curtains draping the floor to ceiling windows. I'm shocked but I really shouldn't be, he fits this room.

*We* fit this room. At least we could, given half a chance, but the way today is going I'd say that's wishful thinking.

Rhys leaves me standing near the door and crosses to his closet, where he pulls out a suit and lays it on the bed before turning back to select a shirt and tie. I scowl, wondering why he is dressing up for the occasion, but I say nothing as he quietly and quickly dresses. When he's ready, he crosses back over to me and takes my hand. "Ready?"

"Not in the least," I reply and he offers me a small, but consoling smile.

He leads me back to the hall, stopping at the console table and pulling a small white paper bag from the slim drawer and tucking whatever it is into his inside breast pocket. Puzzled, I follow him out.

When we step into the elevator, our reflection in the full-length mirror tells me why he changed into a suit for this. We look strong. United. My hope that the move was to send Lisa a clear message blooms. We ride the elevator in silence, although Rhys keeps our fingers entwined and continues to stroke his thumb over my knuckles.

We arrive in the lobby and cross the space to the security desk quickly. Too quickly for my liking and I try to slow us down as we approach, almost turning on my heel to get away from the confrontation about to come my way. Rhys stops and turns to me.

"Do you trust me, kitten?" he murmurs, reaching up and tenderly slipping his fingers into my hair to caress the back of my neck, apparently unconcerned who sees our exchange.

I swallow and nod.

"Good." He smiles, leaning forward to press a kiss to my forehead. "It's going to be okay."

"How do you know?"

"Because this is her last play. It's all she has left to try, but unfortunately for her, I saw her coming. She can't win, kitten."

Then without another word, he walks behind the security post, nodding to the guard and opens the door to the control room beyond and I follow.

"I'm sorry, Mr. McAllister, she wouldn't back down, she was drawing an audience," a sweaty guard huffs out while approaching us.

"That's okay, Chris. I'll take it from here."

Chris nods stiffly and gestures toward another door. "She's in there." He grimaces. "And she ain't happy about it."

"Thank you." Rhys heads for the door, stopping outside and turning to me. "Ready?"

I shake my head vigorously. Rhys, the ass, actually smirks. At a time like this! Then he opens the door and drags me into the room with him.

"Rhys!" Lisa shrieks, simultaneously relieved to see him and aghast at my presence. Her face falls, the latter winning out and she snarls. "What is she doing here?"

Rhys approaches her calmly, having gently let go of my hand. I don't feel the loss as a rejection as I might have expected, rather as an act of protection. After all, there is no need for both of us to approach the cornered beast. "Charlotte is with me but that is none of your concern, Lisa. I made it clear you are not to come back here did I not?"

Her face hardens at his proprietary comment about me being

here 'with' him, but in only a half second it softens again when she looks imploringly at him. "I had to see you, we need to talk and you aren't answering my calls."

"We have nothing left to say to each other."

"That is where you are wrong," she spits, glancing at me with a look of triumph before returning her gaze to Rhys.

"Oh?" Rhys crosses his arms across his chest impatiently.

"I'm not discussing our private matters in front of—*her*," she snaps.

"It's here and now, or not at all," he responds without missing a beat. So calm and yet so firm. "Charlotte isn't going anywhere. Now say what you have to say, I'm a busy man."

"Trust me. Rhys. This is not something you want your new fuck toy hearing." She leans around him, glaring at me. "You can run along darling, we—"

Rhys holds up his hand to stop her and divert her challenging stare. "Do not dare to compare what I have with Charlotte to the arrangement you and I once had. I assure you it is entirely different."

My stomach turns over at the reference to what they 'once had', but Lisa continues, ignorant to my turmoil.

"Until you get bored of her," Lisa scoffs.

"That won't happen."

"Oh please. You'll get restless, you always do. You'll come and find me."

"I feel like you aren't really hearing me, Lisa. So listen, and listen good. We had an arrangement, you and I, nothing more. It suited us both at the time and it ran its course. It's finished now and has been for a while. I've met someone, she's everything. I'd marry her tomorrow if she'd have me."

I gasp, fully aware that it was aloud and clutch my hand in my blouse.

Rhys continues undeterred, delivering the final blow. "And nothing you can do or say is going to change that."

I hold my breath. Silence stretches out for I don't know, a year maybe? Or probably just a couple of seconds, but long enough for me to feel light headed from lack of oxygen.

Rhys is stock still and waiting, Lisa is furious looking and breathing as if she ran here. She glances back to me before squaring her shoulders and fixing him with a vindictive glare.

"I'm pregnant."

Everything stops. Lisa stares expectantly, Rhys doesn't move a muscle and I...well I suddenly need to be anywhere but here. Slowly and silently I feel behind me for the doorknob. I just need to escape. There is nothing left for me here. Rhys is going to be a — I can't even think the word. Not when he's just said he'll marry me if I'll have him.

His life is going to change for good and there isn't a place in it for me. I'm not sure there ever really was. My hand makes contact with the knob, but as I slowly turn it, Rhys' movement stops me.

He reaches into his breast pocket and slides out the small bag, pulling a box from it and screwing the paper up tightly in his fist and flinging it toward the trashcan. It's the only outward hint of frustration he shows. Then he tosses the box on the table between them and looks up at her. "Prove it."

I watch them, confused and then look down at the box. A pregnancy test? But how?

Lisa looks traumatized. "Rhys!" she cries, outraged, his name alone conveying her shock and displeasure at being questioned, suspected.

He unfolds his arms, leaning forward and placing them on the table, looking up into her indignant eyes. "It's very simple, Lisa. If you're pregnant, prove it. Go take the test right now and if it's positive, you'll have my full and unwavering support until we can test for paternity."

She looks down at the box as if it were a snake ready to strike, then back to Rhys.

"Unless you can't prove it," he says low, and I know without seeing his face that the same cold look I saw cross his face upstairs, must be present right now too. Lisa's expression confirms it. She looks terrified. Rhys straightens to his full height before refolding his arms. "In which case, you'd be wise to get the fuck out and never let me run into you again."

She gulps.

"Which is it going to be?" he demands.

Lisa opens her mouth to say something, then changes her mind. Her eyes roam the ceiling for the briefest of moments and then she seems to snap. She grabs her purse from the table and marches past him, stopping in front of me because I'm blocking her path. I hastily move aside.

"Ugh!" she explodes, yanking the door open and letting it fly back on its hinges, crashing into the wall. And with that she storms out. Out of the control room, out of the building, out of our lives.

Rhys approaches me cautiously. I turn to face him, my emotions warring with my better judgement. This man is god damn trouble with a capital T, I tell myself. Everything in your life has turned upside down since he entered it, I remind my subconscious. You wanted a fresh start not a freaking soap opera. *Do the right thing.*

He stands in front of me looking wary, yet maintains his air of confidence. How does he do that when I'm unable to harness any kind of control here?

His expression softens while he waits patiently for me to process.

I can't form a useful thought, but I have to say something. He's waiting for me to say something.

In the end, it's the first thought that cuts through the white noise that's the one I run with, blindly.

"You'd— You'd marry me tomorrow?" I stammer.

A slow grin spreads on Rhys' handsome, confounding, infuriating face. "If you'd have me."

His lips crash into mine before I can reply, his tongue slipping between my lips and coaxing mine into compliance. He growls and grabs me, deepening the kiss as he drags my body flush against his.

A sharp intake of breath cuts into our lust. "Oh. I...uh..." I hear Chris the security guard mutter, more to himself than us and he walks in on our kiss. "Sorry."

Rhys breaks the kiss, his eyes fixed on my swollen lips as he pulls back an inch. He quickly and greedily places another kiss there as if the temptation proved too much to resist. Then he looks up to Chris and smiles, cool as a cucumber. "If she comes back, call the police," he instructs.

"Yes, Mr. McAllister." Chris nods, standing aside when Rhys takes my hand and marches us back through the control room, out across the reception and over to the elevators. We wait in silence until a car comes and we step inside. Up through the floors the silence grows. Then I break.

"So you just keep pregnancy tests on hand?

Rhys laughs, some relief audible. "Not ordinarily, no." He turns to face me. "I just...had a feeling."

"That's a very specific kind of feeling to have," I speculate.

Rhys shrugs. "Let's just say I received a tip off a little while ago that prompted me to be prepared."

I scowl, not appreciating his vagueness at a time like this.

Accurately reading my expression, Rhys concedes. "A mutual friend informed me that she has pulled a pregnancy scam before.

Some heir to a small fortune back in her college days apparently. He finished with her and she tried to sucker him in with an imaginary bun in the oven."

"What happened?"

"He believed her of course, did the right thing. Had her set up in a nice apartment and drowning in luxury before there was any hint it was all a lie. I imagine she milked him dry before she was exposed. I don't know all the details. I just know enough to have been ready for her lies."

I breathe out a long sigh, relieved beyond belief that he has a reasonable explanation and even more still that I actually believe it.

I'm still slightly speechless when the elevator arrives at the penthouse floor. I let him usher me back into his home and right into the bedroom, where he strips off his tie and tosses it to the floor, then sits on the edge of the bed.

Long moments of silence follow and I find myself with the urge to fill the gaping void in conversation.

"Rhys, I—" I blurt.

Only to be cut off by his equal and opposite, "Kitten, I—"

We both stop ourselves and wait expectantly for the other to continue. After a beat, Rhys laughs, standing and taking my hand, walking me over to the huge windows that make up one wall of the room.

We stop and look out at the view outside, the lights of London making the sky twinkle in the twilight. Rhys buries his face in my neck from over my shoulder, laying a tender kiss there.

"Do you think we could wipe that little fiasco from the slate?" he murmurs against my skin.

I blow out an incredulous sounding breath.

"Seriously," he insists. "We were getting somewhere before that happened. I want to pick up where we left off."

His kisses turn to nibbles and I groan, despite myself.

"You were going to tear down that wall remember?" he whispers hoarsely, before taking my earlobe between his teeth.

"Mmmmm," is all I can manage in response.

He threads his fingers through mine, deepening our connection and I feel myself giving in, ready to give it all to him.

He pulls back suddenly, letting go of my hand and unhooking the curtains, closing us off from the world. He comes back to me and stills, raking his eyes over me hungrily. "Take off your dress," he commands.

My heart starts hammering in my chest, unprepared for him to turn the heat up so soon after my chest had been filled with icy fear downstairs. Not ready to pick back up where we were held an hour ago when I'd been consumed with the need to let him help me to let go. Now it seems more than ever that I should keep hold of that control to protect myself.

And yet, I reach behind me, finding the zipper at the back and unzip it slowly, shrugging out of it and letting it drop, pooling at my feet.

"Come here," he demands. His voice hitches, betraying his need, but I obey.

He holds out his hand and I place mine in it, aware that I'm trembling. I step up to him and he drags me against his hard body. I gasp and while my lips are parted in shock, he takes his chance and kisses me so deeply that my legs buckle with the onslaught of passion. He lowers me to my knees before him and then breaks off the kiss.

I groan at the loss.

"Hold out your hands, kitten."

I lift them up slowly, not sure what's coming next, and to my surprise he wraps the cord from one of the curtains around my wrists, just tight enough that I can't break them apart.

"What are you doing?" I ask on a shaky breath.

"I'm helping you, kitten."

"Helping me with what?"

"Finding your saorsa," he whispers. "You've held on to control for far too long. I'm going to show you what it is to be free. You just have to trust me and let go."

And after staring up into his intense eyes for long moments, I know I can do just that.

# EPILOGUE

## Rhys

"Happy birthday, mate," I say as I clink glasses with Michael. It's late and we've moved onto the top shelf. I swirl the single malt we are enjoying in the glass and watch it rise and then die down.

"Thanks." He looks across the bar to where the ladies are dancing to the music with Connor. "Another year older. Still no wiser."

I chuckle. He seems distant tonight. We haven't been friends for long but over the weeks that Charlotte and I have been together, I've gotten to know him quite well. And tonight he seems to have slipped inside himself in a way I haven't seen before.

I know it's thoughts of his wife pulling him there, but he himself has admitted that it's time he stopped allowing that to pull him down. He usually lets thoughts of her lift him up these days, but a birthday can make you reflective I guess.

"You're wiser than all of us," I assure him. "You have Katie to show for that."

His expression softens when he thinks about his daughter. "You're right about that."

"She's an awesome kid, you should be really proud."

"Thanks." He smiles. "I am."

"If you ever want to, you know hit the town, you can always leave her with us."

Michaels eyebrows lift.

I shrug. "We could use the practice." I can't help the smirk I know breaks out. I've been fighting a persistent grin all day.

"Wait. Are you guys thinking of—?" Michaels eyes go wide. I'm sure he probably thinks we haven't been together long enough to even dream of starting a family, but we are way ahead of him.

"She's pregnant." This time my grin almost splits my face and there's no controlling it.

"Holy shit, man!" Michael booms. "Well congratulations!"

I wince and hiss, "Keep your voice down. She doesn't know I know."

Michael frowns. "Huh?"

"She hasn't admitted it to me yet," I clarify.

"Then how do you know?"

I watch her dancing with Louise and Connor and smile. "She was sick for days wasn't she? But it was nothing she ate because I wasn't sick. And it wasn't a virus because I didn't catch it and trust me there is no way I am not sharing germs with that woman."

"Okay...but that doesn't necessarily mean..." Michael tries tactfully to ease me out of my huge assumption.

"And she has been cagey, like really cagey. Hushed phone calls to Louise and some appointment she had right in the middle of the day last week. It was 'nothing to worry about' apparently, but I figured it out."

"But, Rhys, it could have been for anything."

I ignore him, pressing on. "And have you noticed how Louise is trashed right now and Charlotte looks as sober as my granny in church on Sunday?"

Michael studies them. "I guess…"

"She's been drinking all of Charlotte's drinks for her so no one notices she's on the water." I nod sagely. Oh yeah, I've got it all figured out.

Michael looks for the first time like he believes I'm on to something and turns to me wide -eyed. "So why do you think she hasn't told you, if she is?"

"She probably thinks I'll freak out."

"And…you're not freaking out?"

I smile and shake my head. "Not in the least. I'm over the fucking moon."

"Shit." Michaels smiles too. "You've got it bad, my friend."

"Yep, it's terminal," I agree.

"You're a better man than me. I freaked out when I found out about Katie and she was planned. I don't think I could be as calm as you about an accident like this."

I turn to him. "Who said it was an accident?"

Michael scowls. "You mean you've been trying?"

I shrug. "We sure as hell haven't been trying not to. We've never used a condom. The first time we were so out of control it completely slipped my mind. After that she told me she was on the pill, so no harm done. I should have been pissed with myself, but if I'm honest I think I wanted to put a baby inside her." Michael winces slightly and sips his whiskey, but I press on with my TMI. "I know, could I be more of a caveman? I've been trying to decide how soon I can convince her to come off the pill ever since. I figure she missed one maybe and doesn't know how to tell me. Plus there was the whole Lisa drama, she probably thinks I'll go all DNA test on her after that shit show."

Michael blows out a breath and looks over to her. "So what are you going to do?"

I reach into my pocket, pulling out the ring I've had for over a week. "I'm going to give her this and tell her she is my whole world. That I want her to be my wife and the mother of my children and that I want her to share my name before we welcome the first of them. I'm going to promise to put them first until my dying day and love her with all my heart and soul. Then I'm going to hope to fuck she does the smart thing for once and listens to me."

"Think she will?"

I down my drink and set the glass down on the bar pushing my stool back and getting to my feet. I meet his stunned eyes and grin. "Only one way to find out."

## ACKNOWLEDGMENTS

We want to thank our husbands for putting up with our crazy and supporting not only our friendship with each other but being great friends to us yourselves. We love you both!

Big thanks to JR Gray for being our beta while we found our feet as a duo and mixed our styles into something we were proud of.

Thank you to Virgina Tesi Carey and Mandi Gibala for making our words shine!

And finally our deepest appreciation goes to all our readers, especially our HEA Squad. We couldn't do this without your support and love!

# ABOUT THE AUTHORS

**Kerry Heavens** is a London born indie author, iPhone addict & general ray of sunshine! Kerry writes: sometimes sweet, sometimes not, often funny, always hot, real romance, dirty romcoms and other such smut.

**Heather Shere** is a wife of twenty some odd years and wants you to know that you get less for murder. She's also the mother of two adult shaped kids, who she thinks she messed up just enough to make them highly successful individuals, who are also hilarious.

She has a masters degree in snark and nothing entertains her more than someone who can word battle with her. She considers herself an awesome cook and an expert baker but wants to eat out most days, however nothing is made 'the right way' unless she makes it herself.

When she gets bored she likes to tinker with different hobbies like crocheting, scrapbooking, stamping and card making. Her newest and most fulfilling passion is writing and she welcomes you into the deep dark depths of her mind.

## ALSO BY KERRY HEAVENS

Just Human

Still Human

Still Just Human

Spencer

Will

The C Word

Lucky Scars

## ALSO BY HEATHER SHERE

Honey Bee

Divine Hart

Printed in Poland
by Amazon Fulfillment
Poland Sp. z o.o., Wrocław